THE COMMITTEE

Middle East Literature in Translation

Michael Beard and Adnan Haydar, *Series Editors*

THE
COMMITTEE

A NOVEL

SONALLAH IBRAHIM

Translated from the Arabic by
Mary St. Germain
and Charlene Constable

With an Afterword by Roger Allen

SYRACUSE UNIVERSITY PRESS

First Edition 2001
02 03 04 05 06   6 5 4 3 2

First published in 1981 as *Al-Lajnah*

The paper used in this publication meets the minimum requirements of
American National Standard for Information Sciences—Permanence of
Paper for Printed Library Materials, ANSI Z39.48–1984.∞™

Library of Congress Cataloging-in-Publication Data
Ibrahim, Sun'Allah.
    [Lajnah. English]
    The committee : a novel / Sun'allah Ibrahim ; translated from the
Arabic by Mary St. Germain and Charlene Constable.—1st ed.
      p. cm.—(Middle East literature in translation)
    ISBN 0-8156-0726-1 (alk. paper)
    I. St. Germain, Mary S. II. Constable, Charlene. III. Title. IV.
Series.
PJ7838.B7173 L313 2001
892.7'36—dc21   2001049680

THE COMMITTEE

☉   ∏   E

I arrived at the Committee's headquarters at 8:30 A.M., half an hour before my scheduled appointment. I had no difficulty finding the room reserved for interviews, just off a quiet, dimly lit side passage. An old man in a clean yellow jacket stood before the door. His features radiated the serenity that masks the faces of those who, having found themselves at the end of the road, surrender and retreat from the hubbub of life and the struggle to ride out its trials and tribulations.

The porter let slip that the Committee doesn't usually convene before 10 o'clock. This was par for the course. It annoyed me; I regretted having been punctual, crawling out of bed at the crack of dawn, without enjoying a full night's sleep.

The porter had the only seat, so I stood near him and set my Samsonite briefcase on the floor. I offered him a cigarette and lit one for myself. My heart beat violently the whole time, even though I tried to pull myself together and control my nerves. I kept telling myself that my confusion would lose me the opportunity they were granting me. I simply would not be able to concentrate, although I would desperately need that ability during the upcoming interview.

After a bit, I got tired of standing around, so I picked up my briefcase and walked all the way to the end of the long hallway. I turned and came back, keeping my eyes on the meeting room door, afraid the Committee might have arrived and summoned me. But the porter still sat in his place, staring calmly ahead. He worked his toothless mouth as though chewing something imaginary.

I paced up and down the passageway, looking at my watch from time to time. It was approaching 10:30 when I saw the porter jump to his feet and put his cigarette on the floor under his chair. He turned the handle of the door to the meeting room, opened it cautiously, and then disappeared behind it.

I hurried back to my place near his seat. My heart beat even more quickly than before. I expected he would ask me to enter when he came out, but he didn't; rather, after retrieving his cigarette, he resumed his seat and calmly continued smoking.

Finally, I took matters in hand and asked him affably whether the Committee had arrived.

"Only one of them," he said.

I prompted, "But I didn't see anyone enter the room?"

"There's another entrance."

I continued to stand beside him for half an hour while the Committee members arrived through the other entrance. The porter went to the buffet several times to prepare coffee for them. Each time, I tried to peek into the meeting room, but he consistently made a point of opening the door just enough to squeeze through, so that nothing would be revealed to me.

Once, he emerged from the meeting room carrying a leather shoe in one hand. He summoned the shoe-shine boy, who was standing at the end of the hall, and handed him the shoe. When the boy started to sit on the floor by the door, the porter scolded him and ordered him away to where he had been standing earlier.

I began pacing again, shifting my briefcase from hand to hand. I was tired. I hadn't slept well the night before in spite of having taken a sleeping pill and so a slight headache hovered at the back of my head. I had not foreseen this possibility, although I had done nothing during the whole of the last year except prepare for what might happen today. I did not dare leave to look for an aspirin; the Committee might summon me in my absence.

As I paced, I drew near the shoe-shine boy, who was enthusiastically cleaning the "Committee's shoe." For that's how I thought of it, and I liked the turn of phrase so well I smiled. I saw that he had finished polishing the surface of the shoe, had turned it over, and begun daubing polish on its sole.

I turned and walked back to where the porter sat and set my briefcase on the floor by him. I offered him a cigarette, lit one for myself, and stood there smoking. Soon the shoe-shine boy finished and handed the shoe to the porter, who received it reverently and carried it in. After a while he emerged, carrying a brass tray loaded with empty coffee cups. He took it to the buffet and sat down again.

Because it was almost 11:30 and no one else had joined me, I assumed I was the only one the Committee would see that day. And so it occurred to me that the Committee was already discussing my case. This was a very distressing thought. It meant, quite simply, that they were already forming an impression of me. For many reasons, it was more likely this impression would be negative, which, in and of itself, would decrease my chances of swaying them through a personal appearance. I knew they had plenty of reports on me. Nevertheless, I had understood from the first that my fate rested on this meeting. This did not mean it was I who had pressed for this interview; on the contrary, I had been told there was no alternative. And so, there I was.

At exactly noon, the porter went into the meeting room, came right back out, and asked my name. Then he motioned me in.

I took my briefcase in my right hand and fingered my necktie with the left to be sure it was straight. Assuming a confident smile, I placed my hand on the white porcelain doorknob, which I had looked at dozens of times in the last three hours. I turned it, pushed, and entered the meeting room.

Right off I erred on two counts.

In my confusion, which I vainly tried to hide, I forgot to close the door behind me. Then I heard a female voice nearby say tactfully, "Please close the door."

I turned scarlet and went back to the door. Grasping the knob in my left hand, I pushed, but it wouldn't latch.

The door was old and required some pressure to close. I had my briefcase in my right hand, so I pressed with my knee. Sweat trickled down my forehead.

Then I heard the same tactful voice say, "Put the briefcase down and use both hands."

I realized I had lost the first round.

I had known the Committee would question me. Its goal wasn't limited to probing the breadth of my knowledge, but extended to finding the key to my personality and the caliber of my mental abilities. The content of the answer wasn't everything, although it did carry some weight. Rather, assertiveness was paramount.

As I have already said, I spent the past year preparing for this day in all kinds of ways. I devoted myself to studying the language the Committee uses in its interviews. I reviewed all I knew about various fields of learning. I reread philosophy, the arts, chemistry, and economics. I set myself hundreds of inconsistent problems, spending days and nights in search of answers. I followed quiz shows on television and consulted the equivalent sections of newspapers and magazines. Luck was on my side when I discovered that my brother, twenty years older than I, still kept a complete set of *Believe It or Not.* In a package held together with rubber bands, he had kept every issue since its first publication thirty years ago.

Not satisfied with this, I tried to form a clear idea of the Committee's work by searching out others who had appeared before it. Although I was sure there were many, I could only get in touch with a few. Most denied ever having gone before the Committee, or even denied all knowledge of its existence. The rest used the excuse that they had forgotten the details, so their reports were vague and contradictory. I got other tidbits of news from various sources, but they didn't help me either. The only thing I came up with was that there was no set method to the Committee's work.

When I tried to gather information about the Committee members, in hopes of getting an idea of their prejudices and predilections, I found a shroud of secrecy veiling their names and jobs. Everyone whom I asked regarded me with anxious and pitying looks.

However, all agreed that the Committee sets clever traps for everyone it interviews. This means that the tale of the door that wouldn't shut was not a coincidence. It revealed my confusion and lack of resourcefulness even before the interview began.

You can imagine my state after failing this test. I stood before them drenched in sweat. Oddly enough, I sensed, way down deep, a feeling of satisfaction at this failure, as though some part of me feared success. This did not prevent my confusion or my overwhelming desire to gain the approval of those lined up before me at the long table stretching the width of the hall.

There were many of them. Unable to concentrate, I couldn't count accurately. Some of them were absorbed in whispered asides, and others in leafing through the papers before them. Most wore large dark glasses to hide

their eyes. It seemed to me that among them were familiar faces, which had looked out at me at one time or
another from the pages of newspapers and magazines. I
also discovered that I knew the owner of the tactful
voice: an old maid whom I had met on some occasion. I
reproached myself that I had not shown any interest in
her at that time. She looked at me with what I thought
was a friendly smile.

It didn't surprise me to see the military represented
among them. On their collars, red ribbons edged with
gold indicated their high rank.

In the middle of the group was a decrepit old man who
wore thick eyeglasses and held a paper so close it almost
touched them. He was trying hard to read. I surmised
that the paper must be part of a special dossier on me.

The old man finished reading, or perhaps gave up trying, and put the paper down on the table. As he turned
his head to the left, then the right, his colleagues realized that the session had convened. They fell silent and
turned their eyes on me.

I stared at the old man's lips. His sallow face seemed
as remote from life as it could be.

He spoke to me, "At the beginning of this meeting, I
would like to put on record my appreciation, which my
companions share, of your choosing to appear before us.

This does not mean that we will necessarily endorse your point of view. This matter depends on many things, and we are here today to settle it. But what I would like to make clear is that an appearance before the Committee, as everyone knows, is not compulsory. In this day and age, everyone enjoys complete freedom of choice. This choice on your part reflects a high degree of sound judgment and perspicacity. This is an important indicator, which we will take into consideration when we review your case. Only first, we would like to hear your point of view in this matter."

I was aware of what I had heard from various sources: the Committee always requires those it interviews to present the reasons and motives bringing them before it. Therefore, I had prepared an answer in advance.

I had expected the Committee to be on to me, so I thought long and hard before settling on the requisite response. I did not want to present a trite answer, something they had heard before, ostensibly meant to flatter. Rather, I wanted to present a unique answer that would appear simple and spontaneous, as though the question had taken me by surprise. My reply would be reliable and true, giving a precise picture of myself without getting entangled in specifics, such as the true motives of some of my actions. I must allude to these activities so as

to absolve myself of responsibility for everything preju-
dicial to me in the case. I must make them infer what I
imagined would meet with their approval.

In fact, this was an extremely onerous task, given the
highly sophisticated surveillance techniques which they
use to find out everything about me.

Working up my nerve, I took several deep breaths,
then began to speak. My voice could scarcely be heard.
The old man leaned forward, cupping his hand around
his right ear, "Excuse me. I don't hear well with this ear.
Can you speak up?"

I complied with his request and began the answer I
had already prepared. Needless to say, I forgot a large
part of it, as I nervously struggled to speak their language without serious grammatical mistakes.

Nevertheless, I managed to sketch a general picture
of my background, and the way my life evolved under
circumstances which allowed me few options. At the
same time, I was spurred on by grandiose dreams and
the desire to promote my talents and get everything I
could out of them. I made sure I mentioned the standards and moral principles by which I was guided.

After that, I moved on to the misfortune that had
caused my illness. I said that, in all likelihood, my illness was the result of a vast disparity between ambitions
and actual abilities, leaving me fed up with everything,

to the point where I had no option but to change my life completely.

I added a well-rehearsed dramatic flourish to my speech: opening my briefcase, I took out a sheaf of testimonials which I had obtained from various sources, extolling my abilities and confirming the accuracy of the information I had presented.

Since most of these documents were in Arabic, I began to speak about them in the Committee's language. They listened to me with interest, while sorting through the papers I had just given them. I noticed that a fair-complected and light-eyed member seated at the old man's left paid no attention to the testimonials. He was absorbed in examining a file that undoubtedly contained secret reports on me.

A short, ugly member seated on the chairman's right, between him and an officer, looked up and addressed me with hostility, "I can't understand you. After all the progress you've made, here you are trying to start over. Don't you think it's a little late for this?"

I answered him brightly, "Indeed, most people start a new life at forty. This isn't a new beginning in the strict sense of the word, but rather the culmination of the earlier stages of life's journey, a complete blossoming of the diverse potentials I possess. From any angle, it can be considered a natural evolution of my personality."

Stubby snorted angrily. I was taken aback by his rancor. I had a vague feeling that I might have antagonized him by demonstrating my talents and even going so far as to offer proof in the form of those testimonials from respected and influential parties.

I continued this train of thought and came to the conclusion that perhaps as a young man he had stood in my shoes. The Committee must have given him its stamp of approval, but apparently he had failed to live up to expectations. It would seem that in the end he got no further than being merely one of its members. Notwithstanding the Committee's importance and its extensive influence, some, including me, consider membership in it evidence of withering talent and complete failure.

One of the ladies, elderly and dignified, spoke. She was seated at the far left, near an obese man wearing a white jacket, his legs crossed, his head thrown back, gazing at the ceiling as though he were not with us. She asked me, "Do you know how to dance?"

"Yes, indeed. Of course."

Stubby butted in, "Show us, then."

"What sort of dancing?"

I realized this question was a mistake. What sort of dancing, indeed! As if there were any other.

Without hesitation I acted, hoping speed and finesse

would testify on my behalf. Finding nothing else, I took my necktie and wound it around my waist just above my hipbones, right where it would emphasize the body's flexibility. I made a point of putting the knot on the side, as professional belly dancers do. I soon discovered that worn this way, it had a great feature: it separates the belly from the backside, allowing each independent movement.

I began to undulate, lifting my ankles a little off the ground. Glancing down at them over my shoulder, I raised my arms above my head and twined my fingers, framing my face with my arms. I danced energetically for a little while, making an effort to snap my fingers, even after linking my index fingers. I was so absorbed I didn't notice the impression I made on the members.

The chairman, who heard not and saw not, spoke suddenly, motioning with his hand, "Enough."

At that point, one of the officers, his face almost completely hidden behind large dark glasses, leaned forward and said, "We know almost everything about you from the papers before us. However, there is one thing we still don't know, which is, Where were you during 'that' year? Could you please tell us?"

I managed to stay busy removing my tie from my waist and retying it around my neck while thinking about the year he referred to. From what I knew of the

Committee's language, the demonstrative pronoun he had used did not refer to the current year. Since he hadn't mentioned a specific year, he must have intended "that." In as much as I couldn't imagine any omission in the report about me, this had to be a trap.

I couldn't ask for a clarification of the year intended without springing the trap. It was imperative that I figure it out for myself, and as quickly as possible.

To me, the question was of the utmost difficulty. I decided the one way out was to exclude, on the basis of my age at the time, some of the probable years, such as '48 and '52, so narrowing the field of discussion. There remained the years '56, '58, '61, and '67. A concise answer occurred to me before hopelessness set in: one that did not deviate from the truth by much, but still was not comprehensive.

"In jail," I said.

Though short, my answer dumfounded them. No one asked me anything. Part of the hostile atmosphere confronting me at the beginning cleared, or so I imagined. I was at a loss to interpret the look I'd seen in the Blond's light-colored eyes. Was it perhaps mocking?

I saw him note something with a red pen on the paper before him and lean toward the old chairman to whisper something in his left ear, his hearing ear. Then he handed the paper to Stubby.

The chairman addressed me sternly, "We have heard a long speech from you on your talents and abilities. However, we have reports here saying you couldn't perform with a certain woman. This report is unquestionable, since it was submitted by the very woman exposed to this inadequacy. So what do you have to say about it?"

This question took me by surprise. I felt confused. This unwonted episode hadn't happened with just one woman, but with several, and for a variety of reasons. Since the Committee was painstaking in its work, my answer must be specific. But how could it be when I didn't know which woman they meant?

Stubby, motivated by malice, saved me from answering. Unable to control himself, he shouted, "Maybe he's impotent."

But the Blond didn't share that opinion. He leaned over to the chairman's ear and said, "He's probably . . ."

I didn't hear the rest of the sentence, but I had no difficulty guessing.

The Blond motioned for me to come forward until I stood before him. Then he ordered me to take off my pants, so I did. I laid them over the back of an empty seat, then stood before the Committee in my boxer shorts, socks, and shoes.

They kept looking at me as though waiting for something. I pointed to my underwear, "These too?"

The Blond nodded. I removed my shorts and put them on top of the trousers. Meanwhile, their eyes settled attentively on my naked parts.

Next the Blond asked me to turn my back. Then he ordered me to bend over. I felt his hand on my naked buttocks. He ordered me to cough. At that moment I felt a finger inside my body.

After he withdrew his finger, I straightened up and faced them again. I saw this blond man look at the chairman and say triumphantly, "Didn't I tell you?"

The old man smiled for the first time. Everyone burst out talking simultaneously. Commotion filled the hall and I couldn't make out anything they said. Finally, the chairman pounded on the table with his fist to cut off the chatter. When the tumult had subsided completely, he turned to me and said, "Whether we consider events major based on their number and magnitude, or based on their future ramifications, we undoubtedly live in the greatest century in history. By which momentous event among the wars, revolutions, or inventions will our century be remembered in the future?"

I welcomed this question, in spite of its difficulty, because I found it an opportunity to demonstrate my knowledge of subjects especially interesting to me.

"This question is well worth asking. I can cite many matters of such gravity."

The Blond interrupted, explaining, "We want only one thing: that it be international and that it embody the notable and timeless concepts of this century's civilization."

I smiled, "This is the difficulty in a nutshell, your honor. We could mention Marilyn Monroe. This American beauty was truly an international cultural phenomenon, but a fleeting one, which ran its course. Under the influence of the gifted, such as Dior and Cardin, the standards of beauty change every day. Human beings themselves are transitory, which characteristic leads us to eschew the soon to be depleted Arab oil. We might also mention the conquest of space, except that it has yet to bring about anything of value. The same standard makes us eliminate many revolutions, although it may occur to us to pause at Vietnam. However, this is not advisable, since it would lead us to unnecessary ideological complications.

"I say all this because you requested a motif by which our century would be remembered in the future. However, to serve as a motif, the phenomenon itself must still be found in the future.

"If we go in another direction, we can find the right road with no trouble. It is, unfortunately, a long, crowded road, like the Cairo airport road, with its billboards displaying in large letters brand names such as

Phillips, Toshiba, Gillette, Michelin, Shell, Kodak, Westinghouse, Ford, Nestle, and Marlboro.

"I suspect you agree with me, your honors, that the whole world uses these brand-name products. Just as the giant corporations producing them, in turn, use the world, transforming the workers into machines, the consumers into numbers, and countries into markets. Thus, these products are the alarming results of our century's scientific and technological achievements. Furthermore, they will neither perish nor be exhausted, having been created to last.

"Which do we choose then?"

I paused, keeping them on tenterhooks, and looked at them. Then I answered dramatically, "Not one."

A muttering arose among the members. I ventured to raise my hand and say, "Wait a moment, your honors. I didn't mean I am unable to answer the question this revered Committee has posed, but rather I mean to say that the answer is not among the names I gave you."

I paused a moment, then continued, "In response to your question, your honors, I will say just one word, although some would consider it two: Coca-Cola."

I expected to hear some comments from which I could gauge the effect of my answer, but all were silent, so I went on with my speech.

"We will not find, your honors, among all that I have

mentioned, anything that embodies the civilization of this century or its accomplishments, let alone its future, like this svelte little bottle, which is just the right size to fit up anyone's ass."

I smiled, waiting for them to acknowledge my attempt at humor. They continued looking at me blankly, so I went on, "It is found nearly everywhere, both north and south, from Finland and Alaska to Australia and South Africa. Its return to China after a thirty-year absence is one of the headlines which will shape the history of the century. While the words used for God and love and happiness vary from one country to another and from one language to another, 'Coca-Cola' means the same thing in all places and all tongues. Furthermore, its ingredients will not run out, for they can be easily cultivated. People won't give up this palate-tickling taste because of its power to create a habit that approaches addiction.

"Since its advent, Coca-Cola has been linked with the major trends of the age, sometimes sharing to a large extent in their formation. The American pharmacist Pemberton synthesized it in Atlanta, famous as the capital of Georgia, the birthplace of the American president Carter and of the notorious Ku Klux Klan. This was during 1886, the very year in which the famous Statue of Liberty, that symbol of the New World, was completed.

"As for the bottle, it was one product of an American 'war of liberation.' Having vanquished the Indians, the United States plunged into the Spanish-American War in Cuba, which ended in 1899, with the proclamation of 'independence' for Cuba, Puerto Rico, and the Philippines. An American soldier, who, coincidentally, had the same name as the great American philosopher of the preceding century, Benjamin Franklin, saw a bottle of a carbonated beverage made from banana syrup. On returning home, he obtained bottling rights for a new product. The bottle's shape varied until it finally stabilized in the universally recognized form of 'a girl with an hourglass figure.'

"It may have been Coca-Cola that first shattered the traditional image of the ad, previously a mere description of a product. Thus it laid the cornerstone of that towering structure, that leading art of the age, namely, advertising. Certainly, it broke the long-standing illusion of a relationship between thirst and heat through the slogan: 'Thirst knows no season.' It was ahead of its time in the use of radio and neon for advertisements. It sponsored television shows, produced films, and backed new international stars and idols such as actors, the Beatles, and the pioneers of rock and roll, the twist, and pop.

"Coca-Cola went through two world wars and emerged from them victorious. It sold five billion bottles during the seven years of World War II. Then it slipped into Europe under the wing of the Marshall Plan, which backed the war-weakened European currencies by means of American products and loans.

"It then took its place as a leading consumer product, along with Ford cars, Parker pens, and Ronson lighters, but still kept its finger on the pulse of today's ever-changing world. With the advent of the great age of installment plans, and neighbor competing with neighbor for the newest model car with the largest trunk, capable of holding enough groceries to fill the largest fridge, Coca-Cola marketed the family-sized bottle, the 'Maxi.'

"When the United States cooperated in a new 'war of liberation' in Korea, Coca-Cola created the tin can, in order to parachute Coke to the troops. The image of an American opening a can with his teeth has become a symbol of manhood and bravery. However, the can's importance is not limited to this image or the way in which it displaced the bottle during the subsequent Vietnam War, but is outweighed by something more significant. It inaugurated the age of the 'empty': a container to be discarded after its contents have been consumed.

"Without doubt, the success of Coca-Cola goes back primarily to the excellence of the organizational structure it pioneered: the pyramid. The original company comprises the tip, and the independent bottlers and distributors come below it, forming the base. At first, this unique structure enabled it to obtain the necessary financing to saturate the American market. Later, it helped the company avoid Roosevelt's campaign against monopolies and finally allowed Coca-Cola to infiltrate the world. In opening world markets, the company relied on establishing independent franchises headed by well-known local capitalists in every country. This practice produced astounding results. Most strikingly, the American bottle came to symbolize indigenous nationalism.

"Perhaps you have heard the story of the Japanese man who trembled with joy when he was served a bottle of Coca-Cola in a Paris restaurant. He really believed the restaurant's management had especially honored him by flying in his national drink from Tokyo.

"To further illustrate the bottle's significance, let me draw your attention to the article published in the Nov. 2, 1976 issue of the well-known French newspaper *Le Monde Diplomatique.* It mentioned that the president of Coca-Cola, in cooperation with a number of other presidents of large American corporations, had long been grooming Jimmy Carter as a candidate for president of the United States.

"Ladies and gentlemen, this article, which you have

undoubtedly read, says that the presidents of the companies mentioned above created a committee of ten politicians, among them the American president himself and his vice president, Walter Mondale. They represent the American branch of what is called the Trilateral Commission, founded by David Rockefeller in 1973. Professor Zbigniew Brzezinski, national security advisor to the American president, managed it until very recently. It is called the Trilateral Commission because it united North America, Western Europe, and Japan for a specific goal—to confront the third world as well as leftist forces in Western Europe.

"If Coca-Cola has been so influential in the greatest and richest country in the world, you can imagine how dominant it is in third world countries, especially in our poor little country.

"Actually, we are justified in believing what is said about this slender bottle and how it played a decisive role in the choice of our mode of life, the inclinations of our tastes, the presidents and kings of our countries, the wars we participated in, and the treaties we entered into."

The stillness hanging over the Committee seemed to deepen. I decided I might be the cause. Carried away by the subject, I had prolonged my speech more than necessary. But I soon got a feeling that I had "stepped on someone's toes," a common expression in the Committee's language, used to show a person he had inadvertently committed an offense or error.

I was still without my trousers and shorts. I felt completely naked before the Committee, not only in the physical sense, but figuratively, too. I was entirely at their mercy.

The strange thing was, in the last few minutes I had gotten a vague feeling that I could strike back at them, or somehow turn the tables on them.

Stubby cleared his throat. I was beginning to loathe him as much as he loathed me. After seeking permission from the old man, he addressed me in an affected manner, "Your answer reveals the range of your knowledge of current events. We hope you have equal competence regarding historical questions."

The Blond's light-colored eyes gleamed. He said to his colleague Stubby, "If you would permit me . . ."

Then to me, "We will test this point without delay. In view of the importance you gave the pyramidal structure in your speech, let the Great Pyramid be our topic. I don't doubt that you hope to be ensconced at its apex. However, you are absolutely free to start from any point."

At first, I was elated. This was a subject I knew well simply by being Egyptian. I knew it like the back of my hand. However, I had a sneaking suspicion there was a trap here somewhere. I prayed for God to inspire me so I could steer clear of it while also sweeping away any bad impressions caused by my previous speech. He soon answered my prayers. With a flash of insight, I began to speak confidently and calmly.

"The architectural complex of the three pyramids and the Sphinx, erected some five thousand years ago, testifies to the genius of its builders, but is still one of the mysteries that defy human intelligence.

"No doubt, we all followed the American scholar's recent attempt to unravel this mystery by using advanced electronic equipment. It revealed nothing.

"Members of the learned community differ as to how and why the pyramids were built. Among them are those who believe they were built as observatories to record and predict astronomical events. However, Davidson says that the exterior surfaces of the Great Pyramid were designed to reflect light, as would a sundial, and so function as a calendar indicating the dates to sow and reap.

"Of course, most probably, they were intended to immortalize the names of pharaohs and preserve their bodies. Undoubtedly, the obvious goal in building the pyramids was to provide eternal tombs. Even though Cheops, more than any other king in history, succeeded in immortalizing his name, the basic goal of preserving the body was not fulfilled. His body disappeared in spite of the ingenious network of passages and chambers deliberately concealed during construction.

"From Herodotus, we know that the stones used to build the Great Pyramid were moved on the Nile River, then along a causeway built by one hundred thousand workers over a ten-year period. After that, they were raised level by level by means of hoists made of short poles.

"There is no evidence that the Egyptians used mechanical tools more advanced than the hoist and pulley and the incline during any period of their history. Because of this, most scholars tend to believe the size of the building and its precision prove that secret mechanical tools, now lost forever, were used in its construction. Perhaps this was the source of the conflict which arose over the Israelites' role in the construction. Some say that in reality Cheops was an Israelite king, although he concealed the fact in accordance with the customs of that people. Having been unceasingly oppressed since the dawn of history, they maintained complete secrecy in all their dealings in order to protect themselves. Others say that Cheops was only an Egyptian pharaoh, but that he made use of Hebrew genius to solve the knotty problems generated in building this architectural marvel.

"The engineering characteristics of the Great Pyramid prove a thorough knowledge of the science of engineering and a well-developed creativity and originality. These traits were not common in Egypt. Because of this, it is likely that Israelite technical expertise was sought. Some assert that the Israelites were slaves of Cheops and were forced to build the pyramids. This argument is disputed, although it is difficult to deny the despotism of the Egyptian pharaohs through history. However, it is hard to imagine how a structure of such magnitude and precision could result from forced labor. It was more likely the product of a deep faith in a religion which made the pharaohs god-kings.

"Therefore we prefer the theory that Cheops was the secret king of the Israelites. Especially since we know that the engineer who supervised building the pyramid, Ham-Ainu, was Cheops's cousin.

"In any case, this monumental building, composed of 2,300,000 pieces of stone, attests to the genius of its builder. There is some indication that copper saws, each nine feet long, were used to cut large stone blocks. If these blocks were cut into small sections, each one foot long, and placed side by side, they would reach one-third of the way around the earth at the equator.

"It is also certain that cylindrical drills were used to section the stone blocks. In fact, modern drills cannot approach the precision and perfection produced by those of the great builders five thousand years ago. This alone is a true miracle."

I felt the tension clouding the room lift and the hostile atmosphere ease. The Committee members had listened to me with intense interest; even the fat man sitting at one side lowered his eyes from the ceiling for the first time and fixed them on me. When I finished, one of the officers looked at me with approval, which cheered me up. The members stirred and consulted in whispers. Then I noticed I was still naked from the waist down. Tentatively, I reached for my shorts. Since nobody stopped me, I quickly put on both my shorts and trousers.

It seemed that they had finally settled on the opinion the pale man had whispered in the chairman's good ear. Indicating the papers I had given them, he said, "You may take these things now. We have no questions. When we reach a decision, we'll let you know."

I picked them up, trying to appear confident of the decision they would issue, but I had butterflies in my stomach. Drained of all feeling, I moved mechanically. I stuffed the papers into my briefcase, closed it, and took it in my left hand, bearing in mind what had happened to me at the beginning of the interview. I bowed silently to the Committee and headed for the door. I grasped its handle with my right hand and was delighted when it opened easily. I left the hall, not forgetting to close the door behind me, set my briefcase on the floor, and eagerly lit up a cigarette.

I knew I would not enjoy a moment's peace, sleeping or waking, until the Committee had issued its final decision in my case.

T W O ⊙

Several months had passed since the interview, during which time I had fallen prey to shifting moods of hope and despair. I would awake mornings absolutely certain the Committee would decide in my favor. Within hours doubt would begin to gnaw at me, and I would relive every moment of the interview. Then, giving up altogether, I would slide into complete hopelessness.

There was no way to find out where the Committee stood concerning me or where its deliberations would lead. It even occurred to me to try to see that single woman on the Committee, but I couldn't imagine she'd be so foolish as to come right out and tell me what I wanted to know. To get this information I'd have to go too far, and remembering her sallow face, I lost all desire to meet her. Although I had been involved in several things at odds with my principles in one way or another, such as submitting to the humiliation I had suffered at the "hand" of the Committee, I hadn't sunk quite so low as to lead a woman on with false flattery. It wasn't a matter of a reasoned decision, as much as a psychological bent. Even if I could do such a thing, what would save me from having to go all the way? In view of my past history, which the Committee had ridiculed, that would surely turn into a disaster.

There was nothing to do but wait. I hung around the house, rarely going out in case the Committee sent me its decision, whether yea or nay, or summoned me.

I was about to eat dinner one evening, when I received a confusing telegram. Instead of a summons or a brief notification of the final decision, it contained these words, "We await a study on the greatest contemporary Arab luminary."

My slight knowledge of the Committee's methods indicated that I faced unique, unprecedented procedures. The Committee's custom was to determine in one and only one interview the fate of anyone whose luck had led him before it.

This strange reversal of tradition could only be explained by assuming there was a split decision in my case. The new assignment must have been motivated by the strength of my position. The Committee undoubtedly intended it to persuade my opponents (among them, certainly, the ugly Stubby) and to give me a fresh opportunity to display my talents.

This interpretation raised my morale only until I realized there was another side to the coin. On the contrary, why couldn't it be the weakness of my position that made the Committee grant me a second opportunity in order to satisfy those holding out on my behalf? Based on this, the assignment probably wouldn't be particularly worthwhile, being merely a pretext to stall the decision that had already been reached.

Before I despaired completely, a third likelihood occurred to me: that the Committee had incorporated some change in its procedures. I hadn't heard of it, of course, since newspapers give the Committee a wide berth.

I was inclined to accept this explanation, because the requested study would be presented in writing and so would show how well I knew the Committee's language. The Committee had not previously been interested in this aspect of its interviewees' talents.

After that I examined the telegram, looking for the traps for which the Committee was notorious. I found plenty of them. First, the study didn't have a set time or length. Did they want a quick sketch such as is published in the newspapers, or an academic study hundreds of pages long? Likewise, "luminary" was not defined. Could it mean fame, or specific achievements, and if so, what type? And at what level: personal or public, and in what field?

It wasn't possible to consult the Committee. Even if it were possible, it would only make me look inept and ruin my chances, since the Committee puts so much emphasis on the way its questions are interpreted. Better to rely on myself.

I consulted a dictionary and found that in the Committee's language, "luminary" has one meaning: having the characteristic of reflecting light. But in Arabic, it has multiple meanings. It is used to mean lighting and lightning; to mean theft, as in "light fingered." Likewise they say of a pregnant woman: "She glows," and also for someone with exceptional intelligence: "He's brilliant." But the most "luminous" can be the one most given to lying. Apparently the current popular expression "the original shine" is derived form this latter meaning. This phrase first became famous as the brand name of a new shoe polish and then over time evolved into an epithet for anyone addicted to deception, exaggeration, and pretense.

You can imagine my confusion, for the Committee could intend any of these meanings. Which should I look for among the hundreds of personalities who make an incessant racket either in a particular Arab country or throughout the whole Arab world?

I mulled this over for a while, without getting anywhere. Finally, I decided to consider some well-known
local names in various fields, without setting standards
for a decision. By eliminating one after another I would
pare down the search to a limited number of names and
criteria. Then I could make up my mind as to the final
standards of selection.

I began with political leaders and rulers. No one
makes as much noise as they do. But I soon saw the
problems that would result from selecting any of them.
As is well known, they are subject to controversy. In a
study like mine, I must assess the personality and I
might take a point of view contrary to the Committee's.
I could avoid this by choosing another topic.

I decided to eliminate leaders and rulers. When I
could not bring to mind the name of one military
leader, I rejected them too. Then I cut out the poets, because, perhaps mistakenly, I didn't like their high-flown
language and obfuscation. Thus, I was prejudiced
against them from the start and lacked the complete ob-
jectivity such a study required.

I jotted down the names of a number of prominent
writers. But when I began to analyze each one's standing, I found it arose out of the ideas and principles they
had espoused at some time. After much analysis, I perceived that these writers fell into two groups: one,

whether out of intimidation or fear, maintained silence, even though knowing full well what was going on; the other backed off conveniently and smoothly from its previous causes to the point of disowning them.

I searched in vain for one judge whose name was linked with an honorable stance. On this basis, I also threw out journalists, union leaders, and "representatives of the people."

I discovered that most scientists, doctors, artists, engineers, teachers, and university professors were so busy amassing fortunes that they didn't contribute a thing to their professions. It's true that some emigrants are world famous for their discoveries or inventions. (Although I suspect that in most cases, this is nothing more than a trumped-up claim.) But this happened abroad, after they had grown up and been educated in our midst. Their inventions and discoveries were placed at the service of the foreign country and its people. How then are they tied to their birthplace?

Next I contemplated several singers who enjoy a wide popularity. All Arabs listen to them passionately, whether on a mountaintop, in the trackless desert, or in the heart of a city. But I find the hackneyed words and sentimental tunes they din out distasteful.

I did have a soft spot for the voice of one of the greatest, who had a special genius for staying at the top of the charts. In fact, for more than half a century, he remained there, untouched by the stormy events that shook this country. But by chance, I knew the source of most of the melodies for which he took credit, just as I knew that he paid a number of public relations men something like a monthly salary to keep his name in lights, and that he would mercilessly fight the least sign of a new competitive voice.

I spent a comparable amount of time studying the status of those puppets who fill the barren movie and television screens, but I couldn't get enthused about studying any of them in detail. In spite of the precariousness of my position, and my extreme need to gain the Committee's approval, I resolved that in all my affairs, I would only undertake projects that strike a chord in me or that draw a response from something profound or pure within me.

Only the dancers pictured daily in the newspapers remained. Thousands of individuals thirsty for knowledge come from all corners of the Arab world for the pleasure of seeing them in the nightclubs scattered at the foot of the pyramids.

There is something attractive about studying them. By that I mean their remoteness from ideological and political affairs, which in and of itself ensures that I would not aggravate the Committee.

One of them who was constantly in the news flashed across my mind. I had seen her in person only once, by chance, at a nightclub where she was dancing. Even though her movements were not sensuous, I was fascinated by the fleeting glimpses of her lithe, statuesque body, revealed under her shiny, flowing costume. Gifts were showered upon her, and I noticed she had trouble depositing them between her ample breasts. Her costume obviously didn't have room for many of the ten-pound notes the gifts consisted of. The state finally recognized this problem when it issued new one-hundred-pound notes in small, appropriate sizes, thus demonstrating this woman's influence.

I thought about this for a long time. Spending some time alone with her to gather facts for the study appealed to me. She might even allow me to explore the much-used places of her great "art."

Nevertheless, I had to give up this idea, although regretfully. I would meet fierce resistance from the Committee's female members, which would in turn undoubtedly win me some support, at least outwardly, from the other members.

At that point, I felt deeply frustrated and impotent. I saw I was heading for moral bankruptcy and failure. I blamed myself for being led along right from the beginning by a will-o'-the-wisp of ambition developing out

of my exaggerated confidence in my abilities and setting me up for an encounter with the Committee as well
as for further ordeals.

One morning I thought about this. I was nonchalantly looking over the headlines, stopping at some of
them to read the details, with a feeling of bitterness
welling up in me as usual.

A full-page ad on the last page caught my eye. It
showed a scene from the opening ceremonies of a new
American-Arab bank, attended by a number of its senior founders, the majority of whom are prominent personalities.

What caught my attention, to be exact, was the shiny
suit of one man. I hadn't recognized him at first, because of the distortion typical in newspaper pictures. I
only picked him out after reading the names of those
pictured.

His full name sounded strange, because he was
known to me and to most others solely by the title "the
Doctor." Though our countries swarm with thousands
bearing this very scholarly title, its mere mention is
enough to indicate him and no other.

Both his name and title, as well as the shiny suit and
some old memories, kept surfacing in my mind all day.
I had seen him once in person, about five years ago,
when my taxi stopped at a traffic light in Ramses

Square. I saw everyone looking at a magnificent, late-model Mercedes, with our friend seated in the back talking on a telephone. It was odd at the time, because we were still in the aftermath of the October War and weren't yet open to the West. Moreover, how do you suppose a mobile phone could possibly work when most phones in the country were out of order?

A year of so after this, circumstances took me to Baghdad. I had set out with an Iraqi friend through the quiet streets near the city center when I noticed a two-story house across the street, surrounded by a small garden. It was guarded by a number of soldiers wearing camouflage uniforms and armed with automatic weapons. I asked my friend about its owner. He scolded me in a faint voice, looking at the ground, "Look straight ahead, not over there!" I did as he asked and when we were out of range he said to me, "Do you want to do us in? That's the Doctor's house!" I didn't dare pump him at that moment, but I still didn't know whether he meant my well-known countryman or another person, an Iraqi, who contended with him for the title.

Seriously considering this now, I see that it makes no difference whether it's one or the other. Having a rival in every Arab capital doesn't detract from my countryman. On the contrary, this rivalry brings to mind other similarities, if in fact this isn't just one person, and confirms once again the importance of this man and his affairs.

Perhaps you have noticed my interest in this matter. Once I had seen the connections between these memories and impressions, I became increasingly convinced that I had finally found exactly what I had been searching for. The Doctor might not be as well known as the singers or dancers, but he is certainly more powerful and influential than they are, not only within my country but throughout the whole Arab world. Clearly he very much has a hand in shaping the present and the future. How can there be anyone more illustrious than that?

I took matters in hand and made him the subject of the requested study.

I devised a brilliant plan, which was, in short, to read everything written on him: studies and newspaper and magazine articles. Then I would interview him. I would ask a number of clever questions carefully phrased so as to fill the gaps in my reading and complete his personality profile. I intended to describe him accurately and precisely.

I was forced to amend my plan when I couldn't find a single book about him. Apparently no one else had noticed his importance, or found him a gripping subject, or perhaps writers were waiting for his death so his biography would be complete.

As happy as I was to broach a subject no one had dealt with, I knew the difficulties that would result. So I decided to start by interviewing him. He might point out an article that had eluded me, or perhaps might not object if I examined whatever personal papers he might have.

I put on my best clothes and took my Samsonite briefcase. Inside it were a small Japanese tape recorder, a new notebook, some pens, and a slip of paper with the main points I wanted to raise with him.

I hurried to one of the foundations linked with his name, having obtained its address from the phone books. At the information desk I learned that the Doctor didn't keep a regular schedule. When I explained I urgently needed to meet with him, naturally without revealing the real reason, the clerk searched my briefcase for weapons and explosives, then referred me to one of the secretaries.

The secretary gave me the cold shoulder. She told me in no uncertain terms that I wouldn't be able to interview the Doctor in the near future. In the first place, he rarely comes to his office because he constantly shuttles between the Arab capitals on business. Second, there is a long list of people waiting for appointments. Third, I would have to explain my request in full, flawlessly written, so she could forward it to the office manager. I learned from her that he was one of those well-known university professors who had been in the limelight during the '60s and whose names were linked with ambitious projects for heavy industrialization.

I was completely at a loss. I couldn't mention my connection with the Committee. In spite of its importance and the extent of its authority, from an official standpoint it didn't exist. Any attempt to link my request with it would be received with surprise and scorn. While it was possible to bring up the subject with the Doctor himself, it was impossible to allude to it in a memo the secretary would bring to the office manager's attention. If I were to omit the Committee's role, what other reason could I give? "An unknown amateur writer seeks to write a book about your eminence." What would assure him that I was not just some deceitful imposter trying to get a foot in the door to ask for a job or charity?

I left, depressed, to study the matter. Time seemed to fly by without my getting anywhere. Trying to get an appointment with the Doctor could take days or maybe weeks, and might in the end come to nothing. Because of this, I altered my plan a second time and decided to put my nose to the grindstone immediately by beginning to collect everything published about him in the newspapers.

I went along to the huge building that houses the offices of the most important and widely circulated daily newspaper. Since I considered an appropriate point for tracing the Doctor's eventful career to be twenty-five years ago, I asked to see the issues published from that date.

I sat at one of the tables in the reading room and took an empty notebook and a pen out of my briefcase. Meanwhile, the attendant brought me several dust-covered volumes of the newspaper. I picked up the first volume, opened the cover, and began to turn the pages.

I plunged at once into a strange world that came alive in my mind: exciting events, famous men and women, and their boundless ambitions. The images of the past absorbed me, until, with difficulty, I tore my eyes away from the dusty pages and reminded myself of my goal. I turned the next pages slowly and unwillingly. I was like someone recalling his childhood and youth, who despairs when reflecting on the hopes and dreams that had once beguiled him, especially considering how things had turned out.

I got dizzy from turning the pages, shifting my eyes between the headlines and the pictures and inhaling the dust. I realized the enormity of the task I had imposed on myself when, after three hours, I hadn't examined more than ten issues. A familiar sinking feeling came over me. I craved a cup of coffee or a glass of beer, but I couldn't muster enough energy to order anything from the tea boy who peered in regularly to check for customers.

The attendant settled the matter by informing me that it was closing time. I sighed in relief, returned my papers to my briefcase, having written nothing, then picked up my briefcase and left the reading room.

I calculated that if I read the issues I wanted from just this newspaper, there would be 265 x 25 years = 9125 issues. If I worked a normal shift every day without interruption, and without falling ill, or being stuck in traffic, or having the electricity or water go off, or other typical surprises, I would need about one thousand days. That would be three years for just one newspaper.

I couldn't bring myself to rely entirely on one newspaper. Although the national newspapers constantly print the same news and commentary, and even the same pictures, the social and entertainment sections have some diversity. I pinned my hopes on these sections. After all, since he wasn't a political figure or movie star, news about the Doctor wouldn't be in the front-page section.

There were also weekly and monthly magazines as well as the newspapers and magazines published in the East and West. All this means, to be honest with myself, that I would need to be completely free to devote at least three or four years just to gather the material. Then there would be the time required to study and analyze it and draw conclusions.

I wasn't apprehensive about being absent from my real job, since the Committee arranges a paid leave of absence for its interviewees until their cases are finished. However, I was ignorant of the period allotted for the study and consequently I couldn't afford to commit myself to such a time-consuming methodology.

I searched in vain for a solution, until I remembered that one of the largest daily newspapers maintains an extensive archive, which is the pride of its founders and includes detailed information on important Arab personalities. Rumor has it that the Committee has obtained a copy of this archive and relies on it heavily in its work. I assumed that what this archive contains on the Doctor would be of great help to me.

Not just any member of the rank and file is granted access to the archive. I really had to hunt to come across someone to recommend me to its director, after which the said file was at my disposal in no time.

It wasn't as large as I expected. In one corner was the emblem of the publishing house and the complete name of the Doctor, in highly ornamented calligraphy.

I opened the folder, my fingers trembling from excitement. It revealed a white sheet of paper with a date from the early '50s at the top and nothing else. I turned it over and saw a similar sheet of paper.

Quickly, I examined the sheets of paper in the file and saw that they all lacked everything but a date. At the top of each sheet I discovered a trace of the glue that had stuck down clippings from newspapers and magazines.

The clerk in charge was surprised when I showed him the file, but he didn't let me in on anything. I was about to leave when it occurred to me to make a note of the aforementioned dates. I could go back to the newspapers and magazines they came from and so get access to the contents of the file in a relatively simple manner.

I jotted them down immediately and went to the next room to explain my problem to the attendant and get the volumes matching my first date. I was surprised at the lack of anything about the Doctor. When I got to looking carefully, I found small sections had been carefully cut out of the pertinent issues with a razor blade. I noticed that some of them were on the pages devoted to crimes, movies, and television.

I had misgivings about this matter of missing sections. I decided to continue the research to confirm my suspicions. When I returned the next day, I was surprised by a new sign prohibiting nonemployees from using the library.

The same thing happened lock, stock, and barrel at the other newspapers, from the secret razor to a decree preventing me from using their libraries.

I resorted to the National Library and gave the authorities a list of the issues I wanted to see from the daily papers and weekly magazines. After waiting a few hours, I was informed the issues I had requested were currently at the bindery.

I had no more doubts, so I started thinking up a devious stratagem. I went to the offices of one of the weekly women's magazines and asked to see the issues published a week or two before my dates. When the clerk asked what I was working on, I took the precaution of saying I was researching famous crimes in contemporary Arab history. Each week, these magazines customarily cover important incidents and have a "police beat" column for criminal news as well as a separate column for news of the arts.

I dug into my work enthusiastically, my interest kindled primarily by the unexplained phenomena that leapt out at me. Luck was on my side when I discovered a picture of the Doctor as a young man in an issue published close to my first date. There he was—a new face in the film industry, with a successful comedy production under his belt.

Within months of my second date, I came across an

article recounting the details of a strange crime: a young man had attacked "a well-known artistic personality," whom the magazine described as "a dedicated patriot." I extrapolated from the article that this person had something going with the assailant's sister. That very day she had been found dead under mysterious circumstances and her brother suspected this person. Nobody attached any importance to the accusation, so the brother had no choice but to shoot him. However, he wounded him only slightly.

It was strange that during the inquiry the injured party accused the defendant of being a member of a leftist organization, then made up with him and gave him a job in a company he managed.

A little voice kept whispering the real name of this artistic personality. My hunch was confirmed when the article gave his background and mentioned that before the revolution he had been a member of one of the extremist nationalist associations that played a prominent role in the struggle against English imperialism (this is a well-known fact of the Doctor's life), and that he abandoned his studies in 1947 to rush to Palestine at the head of a regiment of his enthusiastic comrades. There they fought in the war against the Zionists, who in turn fought desperately to create an Israeli state. After the revolution, he finished his degree and got involved in producing films.

This discovery cheered me up. I continued working along the same lines and was able to gather some valuable information, although it took quite a bit of time.

I learned that on the eve of the Tripartite Aggression against Egypt, he cofounded a carbonated beverage company, and that he was among those who stepped forward to buy up the foreign companies taken over after the aforementioned attack.

I came across the text of a speech he had delivered during an economic conference held in Damascus in the early days of the UAR He portrayed Arab unity as the lofty calling of every Arab in this century. He also attacked the Communists, accusing them of treason in consenting to the 1947 partition that authorized the creation of two states in Palestine, one for Arabs and the other for Jews.

I found some relatively unimportant, scattered items concerning him from this time period. Then fortune, which only rewards the persistent, smiled on me. By chance I came across a small bit of news in the social column, alluding to the lecture he delivered at a women's club in Algeria on the "Arab concept of socialism." For the first time, I found his name preceded by the title the

Doctor. In an issue dated some months later I came across a full-page statement from a subcontractor in the public sector, congratulating the president of the country on his triumphs. Below it, the Doctor was listed as the director of the firm.

There was a long dry period, until I came across a statement published in the summer of 1967, which referred to a series of articles by him in one of the daily newspapers. The series analyzed the reasons for the defeat and attributed political responsibility for it to the Soviet Union.

During this period, he married for a third time. She was a daughter of an Arab oil potentate, known for her strange caprices and escapades. Naturally, considering the slant of the magazine, news about her soon eclipsed news about him. In the following years' issues, I found only brief hints at extensive achievements and huge projects undertaken in various areas of the region, especially after the October War. In these projects, the Doctor was the connecting link between foreign financiers and local consumers.

I felt that I'd gotten all I could out of the women's magazine, and that it was time to move on. When I thanked the library director for his help, he introduced himself to me.

I was surprised, because his had once been a well-known name among newspaper columnists. I muttered, "But how? . . ."

He answered my brief question, "Ask the one you are researching."

This really got to me and I quickly asked, "Whoever do you mean?"

He smiled, "Don't be afraid . . . I won't say anything at all to anyone."

"I'm not afraid. I'm backed by influential circles I'm not at liberty to disclose."

His smile widened, "I wouldn't blame you if you were afraid."

"How did you know?"

"From you. When you have sat in my place as long as I have, you can tell at first glance the nature of the people frequenting the library to examine old volumes. When I noticed you were different, my curiosity was aroused. It wasn't difficult for me to trace the pages you paused at or to deduce your interest in him."

I continued questioning him, "How did you come to be secluded here?"

"An article I published."

I looked at him questioningly and he added, "You can easily look it up."

I told him about the difficulties hampering me in my search through the daily paper for news of the Doctor.

He interrupted me, "You will certainly find my article, because nobody pays any attention to the newspaper that published it. Besides, I didn't mention him by name."

He gave me the date the article was published and wished me luck. I immediately went to the newspaper. It was an evening daily with limited circulation, which was the reason I hadn't been interested in it at the beginning.

I looked for the article without telling anybody my objective. I stumbled upon it under the provocative title with tragic overtones, "Who Is Removing the Trees?"

Under this title, the writer discussed the disappearance of trees from Cairo's streets and few remaining gardens. Furthermore, he said that from the orderly way they were uprooted, influential persons appeared to be behind it. He asked whether there was a relationship between this phenomenon and the fabricated crisis in the lumber market, which resulted in inflated prices and a black market.

I recorded the contents of the article in my notebook. Then it occurred to me to take the opportunity to proceed in a new direction. I still stuck with this newspaper, but checked specific places: the social calendar, the business section, and the obituaries, at around the same dates I had previously used as a guide.

I hadn't anticipated the amount of information I would come across this way. For example, there was a series of "thank you" telegrams from the Doctor to the president of the country, and another of congratulations to the Doctor from a number of important people. Thus, I learned he had won a seat in Parliament in the general elections.

From a long obituary about some woman related to him by marriage, I discovered an extensive network of relationships linking him to the best-known, richest families and to the individuals holding the top positions in the justice department, the police, the army, the administration, and the world of business and finance.

Advertising, modern man's tool for successful communication, led me to another exciting discovery.

A series of ads caught my eye. They had been published repeatedly on the first page of the paper in recent years, showing French perfume, American cigarettes, and Japanese tape recorders. The advertiser's name was left off, whereas usually in such ads, the name of the importer or "agent" in the Committee's language, the authorized local representative, is mentioned.

The incessant work I had recently undertaken stimulated my mind, as was typical. I began to delve deeply into what came my way, trying to deduce underlying motives and relationships. My curiosity was aroused, so

I went over to the paper's advertising department. I pretended to be a reporter from one of the foreign economic journals, preparing an in-depth report on ads published by the Arab media about foreign products.

The upper management of the department was too busy welcoming me to check my credentials, especially after I expressed my admiration for the successful jingles which advertised perfume and filter cigarettes. After all, the masses repeat them in complete obedience. I won their friendship by jokingly asking who among them hadn't yet switched to filters. This way, I easily got the information I wanted.

I wasn't surprised to learn that the Doctor's oldest son by his first wife managed the local firm that imported these products. I had anticipated something of the sort. But I was truly surprised, so much so that I almost burst out laughing, when they showed me the layout of a full-page ad prepared by that same firm for immediate publication on the last page of all the national papers. The ad promised the Egyptians nothing other than the return of the real Coca-Cola.

T H R E E

I continued visiting the newspaper's premises for some months. The discoveries I made encouraged me to persevere along these lines, especially since no obstacles cropped up.

I came up with a lot of information, several notebooks full. Actually, some of it didn't have any real connection with the Doctor. My interests had gradually and unintentionally expanded to include some general matters. The news items I had previously read now seemed to scroll past my eyes for the first time. It was as though they took on a new significance with the passage of time, which allowed me to see all their diverse interconnections.

At the end of each day, I returned to my apartment exhausted, suffering from dizziness and difficulty in breathing. Dead tired, I would climb the seven floors to my top-floor apartment. After I had bathed and eaten, I dozed a little, then got up to work again. I transferred what I had written down in the morning to index cards provided by a close friend who could not hide his pity. I entered the information under the date the article was published, its source, and the most important subject, in anticipation of sorting the cards to start the second stage of research. I didn't finish until late at night. I slept fitfully, disturbed by unpleasant dreams consisting mostly of newspaper headlines. Once in a while I had a pleasurable dream dominated by images of scantily clad international beauty queens and movie starlets who had caught my attention from time to time.

Preyed upon by depression, I would struggle out of bed in the morning. My imagination multiplied the difficulties I might suffer after reaching the newspaper building and the obscure dangers that surrounded my work. I wouldn't perk up until I had visualized my successes and the remarkable world that had opened up before me.

Actually, a change had come over me in the last months. Formerly I had been bored with everything. My presentation to the Committee and the pursuit of any opportunity that would promote my talents was only an attempt to renew my interest in life. However, the research on the Doctor soon engrossed me, so much so that I began to dread death and prayed that God might avert traffic accidents and heart attacks until I had finished it.

One day when I felt particularly run down, I had to put off leaving. I sat and consulted the index cards I had written out. They were filed in a shoebox to make it easy to retrieve what I wanted.

I found I had a considerable amount of material on my main topics. But I was still ignorant of much of the background of some important points. There was no use in checking the Egyptian or Arabic newspapers, since the political and social situations discourage them from investigative reporting. It occurred to me that foreign magazines might help me, but where could I find collected back issues of even one of them?

The friend who had helped me with the index cards suggested I try the library at the American Embassy. I went to its new location. It had moved there after rioting mobs had burned the old building in 1965. They had been protesting the United States' role in the assassination of Zaire's nationalist leader, Lumumba, and its support of Mubutu, the next leader of Zaire, which was formerly Congo-Kinshasa.

At the library I found scattered issues from better-known American magazines, such as *Time* and *Newsweek*. I leafed through them, concentrating on the pages about the Middle East and disregarding the covers and other parts. Because of this, I didn't notice that one of the issues I held in my hand had a color photograph of the Doctor on its cover. I noticed only afterward, when I found myself trembling with excitement as I read the detailed article about him. It was several pages long and chock full of exciting information.

It was one of last year's issues, covering the wedding of his daughter to an Arab president. This was news to me. Our papers hadn't mentioned it. Apparently, at the time, the marriage had aroused a storm of commentary, not only because of the difference in age, which exceeded thirty years, but primarily for its political and economic implications.

The magazine took this as an opportunity to print a brief biography of him: how he came from a poor family, and how fortune smiled on him when the revolution broke out, because he was related to one of its leaders. This connection set him on the road to success by enabling him to get permission for a movie producer to make three comedies on the army, the navy, and the air force. In return he got a share of the take.

The magazine went on to say that once he had accumulated capital, it was not difficult to double it in a short time. It wasn't his fault that those running the economy, having been carried away by socialist ideas, had tied it up in a way that only special talents and consequently high fees could undo. By means of the extensive relationships he had reinforced through a series of successful marriages, the Doctor profited from removing these difficulties for whomever so desired. But the true beneficiary was the national economy. As an example, the magazine cited his role as a public sector contractor. He steered most of the projects to private companies he co-owned. Whatever the opinion of this practice, he indisputably helped support both private enterprise and the completion of many important public service projects, whose fruits the Egyptians enjoy today. These projects could never have been realized if they had been left up to the public sector.

At that time, the Doctor underwent a rigorous ordeal. The authorities seized him and put him in jail. It is hard to say why, since accounts differ. Rumor has it that he participated in an attempt to overthrow the government, and some said he had gone too far in advocating socialism. Someone confirmed that he was implicated in questionable financial dealings which were then illegal.

The magazine delved into the various rumors about him, describing them as the price paid for success in Arab countries. Its example was the rumor claiming that he attended the famous party held at one of the Egyptian air bases on the eve of the June War in 1967.

According to the article, this rumor didn't mean anything whatsoever, since most Egyptian leaders attended it. As for other rumors attempting to link him with the surrender of the Golan Heights, there was a complete lack of evidence. As proof of his patriotism, the magazine cited his role in the war of attrition, when he won a contract to build gigantic fortifications costing millions of dollars. Rumors continued to fly even while he carried on this noble pursuit.

The magazine also said that when Egypt was liberated from Soviet domination in the '70s, his life entered a new stage as he transferred his activities to supplying arms, a profession which always yields astronomical profits. He became one of the largest suppliers, and so got credit for the victory in the October War. However, the largest profits resulted from the skyrocketing price of petroleum after the war, and so didn't find their way to his pockets; since he failed to attain them through his own short-lived third marriage, he then tried to succeed by marrying off his daughter.

Although the Doctor didn't stop importing weapons for limited conflicts in the Middle East and Africa, and although he made known, more than once, his resolve to form a strong company of mercenaries, ready to serve anybody willing to pay the price, he nevertheless became an advocate of peace. He worked energetically to import foodstuffs, cars, and airplanes, thus benefiting from the open-door policy. In this connection, the magazine cited the statement prevalent throughout the Arab world, "Even if the Doctor doesn't bake the pie, he's first in line for a slice."

The magazine noted the many colorful stories about him. Take for example, the one about the million uniforms leftover from the Vietnam War, which were donated by the United States Army on behalf of poor Egyptian peasants. They found their way to his warehouses, where they were sold in turn to a number of merchants for the equivalent of six million pounds.

It concluded the article by saying, "One can only admire the vitality and energy of this Arab billionaire. This vitality emerged and left its mark on the last decade. In spite of the price terrorists put on his head after his cooperation with Israeli firms became common knowledge, his energy will undoubtedly last a long time before it withers.

"Because of his age, he now needs artificial and chemical aids above and beyond a face-lift in order to carry out his conjugal obligations when visiting his numerous mansions scattered throughout the Arab world. However, he needs no assistance in the financial dealings of political activities he manipulates from behind the scenes. Whatever is said about his moral principles, it cannot be denied that the Doctor and his ilk carry the torch of progress, peace, and stability for the region, which has long been disrupted by extremism."

I entered the whole article in my notebook, which took several hours. Afterward, happy, I returned to my apartment and got busy at once transferring my information onto separate index cards, or, depending on the subject, adding some parts to existing cards.

No sooner had I finished than I felt I had completed my preparations. There was nothing preventing me from starting the second stage of the research.

I was inclined to make his biography the backbone of my work: to begin with his family and childhood, then to move on to his school days and youth, and from there to his patriotic activities. I would continue with his rise to power, which encompassed the three consecutive wars: the Tripartite Attack in 1956, the June War in 1967, and finally the October War in 1973. I would finish with the pinnacle he now occupies in the Arab world.

But I soon perceived the gaps in this program. The information available to me from the first stage of this life was extremely sparse. I had not known until now whether his nickname "the Doctor" was supported by a Ph.D., or whether the appellation was a convention, with nothing original or unique to it. The most important thing in all this was that it put me face-to-face with the question that had to be answered, namely, what comes after a climax? The strong relationship between this question and one meaning Arabs give to "luminous," as in "She glows"—the fetus stirring in the womb—is apparent. The significance of the answer itself is also clear, since his destiny is a simple matter after so much study.

I was so deep in thought I didn't sense it getting dark. When I did notice, I lit the electric light on my desk. At that moment the doorbell rang.

As I had mentioned before, I live on the seventh floor and there is no elevator. In spite of the law requiring owners of apartment buildings with more than five floors to provide an elevator, my landlord was able to get around the law quite easily by building the last two floors set back a little, so that they are not readily visible from the street. This way the law was satisfied and so did nothing, no matter how much we residents complained to the appropriate agencies.

At any rate, this didn't encourage anyone to visit me, which didn't bother me at all. On the contrary, lately it was a course of deep, intense relief since I was so overworked. If anyone did come, he would be compelled to climb the stairs. When he got to the top floor, he would be winded and his footsteps would be heavy. The walls were so thin, due to another attempt by the owner to avoid the clearly defined building codes, that while I was sitting at my desk, even before the doorbell rang, I could distinctly hear footsteps.

I had been hearing footsteps for a while. But because I was so deep in thought, it didn't dawn on me until I noticed how many there were. I was surprised when I opened the door and found so many ladies and gentlemen crowded into the narrow hall in front of my apartment.

The stairs were black as pitch because the landlord had removed the light fixture in an attempt to pressure the residents into withdrawing their complaints. Because of this, I couldn't see the faces of the visitors clearly at first. When I recognized the Committee members before whom I had appeared nearly a year earlier, I was profoundly astonished.

My heart beat violently and I stepped back from the door, saying in confusion, "Do come in . . . Do come in . . . I hadn't expected . . . I hadn't expected . . ."

This was true. I had never ever imagined the Committee might visit me at my apartment. Actually, lately I had been so immersed in my work I had almost forgotten its existence and the real purpose of the study I was so caught up in preparing.

The Committee members didn't wait for a second invitation. They sauntered into my small apartment and immediately scattered throughout it. They looked closely at its contents, poking around behind and under my bits of furniture. That single woman and her elderly companion went over the contents of the kitchen, which was located opposite the front door. Meanwhile, two of the three high-ranking officers closed in on my sturdy refrigerator, a product of Egyptian industry in the '60s, and started comparing it with the new imported fridges.

I closed the door and stood there aghast, unable to comprehend. I looked around for their chairman, the one who couldn't see well and only heard with one ear. I didn't find him and concluded that he either hadn't come with them at all, or couldn't climb the stairs because of his age. I did notice the ugly Stubby and his companion with the light-colored eyes. As had happened the previous time, since I couldn't concentrate, and since I was preoccupied with finding an explanation for their unexpected visit, I couldn't tell how many were there.

In a voice I tried to keep steady and resonant, I said, "Shall I make tea or coffee?"

No one answered me. Silence fell. I watched them assemble in front of the rows of books I had placed systematically on the floor of the hallway leading to the bedroom, then rummage through them. I found this a

great opportunity—one that hadn't crossed my mind—
by which they might detect the scope of my study, especially since the books were in several languages and on a
wide range of subjects.

Stubby suddenly broke away from the group and, ac-
companied by his buddy the Blond, headed quickly for
the inner room where I worked and slept. I hurried
after them.

There were piles of books, newspapers, and magazines all over, but they ignored them, and homed in on
the small table I used for writing. There were some files
and newspapers on one side and a pile of books with a
dictionary on top at the other. In the center was the
notebook I had been working on, and beside it the index
cards I had been using, along with the shoebox contain-
ing the rest of them arranged according to a system I
was proud of.

Stubby walked around the table, sat down, and
leaned over the index cards, looking them over with interest, unable to conceal his excitement. As for his
buddy, he had stopped, stone-faced, to flip through the
files and newspapers.

Pulling a large piece of cardboard from between the
files, he suddenly said, "What's this?"

He was indicating some pictures cut from pictorial
magazines. I had pasted them skillfully onto a piece of

paper so that they appeared to be a single picture. The American president Carter was in the center, facing us, looking over our heads, as suits his lofty position. Right next to him was a very small picture of the Israeli prime minister Begin. I had replaced his long trousers with a child's shorts and the two looked like father and son. In a semicircle in front of them I had pasted a collection of pictures of the more prominent personalities of the Arab world: presidents, kings, leaders, intellectuals, and businessmen, genuflecting as if in prayer, thereby presenting us their rear ends.

I answered, smiling, "This is a hobby I engage in from time to time. I cut pictures of famous people out of magazines and glue them onto cardboard, choosing suitable situations. I add other pictures to complete the situations until I get a perfect scene."

He continued looking at the scene with disapproval. After a moment I added, "As you know, there is a whole school of art whose work is founded on a similar basis. At first this appears extremely simple, but to get worthwhile results you have to successfully link originality and novelty on the one hand with profundity on the other."

He didn't say anything, but put the scene aside as though intending to return to it later and resumed looking through my papers.

Stubby now addressed me, not raising his eyes for a moment from the index cards he was giving the once-over. "We never imagined you could collect so much information. It is as admirable as it is unfortunate."

It didn't surprise me that the Committee knew what I was doing, or that Stubby used Arabic, since I was sure the Committee members had mastered it. But his words really alarmed me. I waited anxiously for him to explain what he meant.

He looked directly at me. I discovered for the first time that he was walleyed, which accentuated his ugliness. He went on to say, "We had thought that the obstacles placed in your path would divert you to another subject. In fact, we were in hopes of that, because . . . because some of our members pinned great hopes on you."

The blood drained from my face and my eyes hung on his ugly eyes. Meanwhile, abandoning the index cards, he pushed his chair backward.

"You can decide for yourself now, whether to persevere or to change your subject. We don't force anyone to do anything."

"After all this time?" I said in agitation. "The year is almost over."

"This is a trivial point. The Committee has the power to give you as much time as you need," he said forcefully.

I clenched my fists. Triumphing over the disgust he

engendered in me, I said in an ingratiating voice, "I've covered a lot of ground and am just finishing up."

One of the officers, who had come into the room during the conversation and so heard part of it, said, "Didn't you think about the significance of what you were doing and its effects?"

Defending myself, I said, "My research was strictly objective. I covered nothing but proven facts and logical explanations. I have almost finished collecting and organizing the required information. I need only distill the important points and weave them into a well-ordered analysis."

"This is precisely why we want to give you some advice," Stubby said angrily.

The rest of the Committee members had begun to congregate near me. The two women sat on the edge of the bed, and one of the officers sat beside them. Next to them, another officer sat on the armchair. The third officer and some other members joined the Blond at the table. Others leaned on the arms of the chair, the wardrobe, and the door. Stubby held out some index cards. Among them I noticed the ones with the notes from the American magazines. They passed them around in silence, then began to look at me. They formed a semicircle surrounding me.

I faced them again imploringly, "I chose the Doctor

after much thought and scrutiny. The selection of the most luminous personality in the Arab world is an exceedingly difficult matter because of the number of countries, the spread of education, the proliferation of communications, and consequently . . ."

Stubby interrupted me angrily, "And consequently the existence of many luminous personalities. You admit to it."

I answered heatedly, "We will not find a greater luminary than the Doctor, or anyone with a stronger presence anywhere in the Arab world. It would be enough that the idea of Arab unity is inextricably linked with his name. He is one of its foremost advocates, as is well known. What most people don't know and what I have clearly documented is that during this decade, when the demand for Arab unity has declined, he is one of its most prominent advocates and dedicated believers. Even more strikingly, the unity, which was not achieved in the period when its popularity was on the rise, is now being realized even as its popularity declines. This is not immediately apparent to the observer faced with the difference and dissentions prevailing between the various regimes. But when he looks deeper, he finds under that misleading exterior a strong unity, the likes of which we have never before witnessed. That unity, for which the Doctor deserves all the credit, is the unity of foreign commodities used by everyone.

"Once again I emphasize that the documents I collected confirm his strong relationship with all the fateful events our nation has experienced during the past thirty years. Today he, more than any person at any time, holds the political threads of the future in his hands.

"It is enough to say that he was the middleman for the huge multinational corporations in providing for our nation the new equipment and inventions that have become part of contemporary civilization, everything from Samsonite briefcases and transistors to electronics and jumbo jets, and from toothpaste and shaving cream to vaginal deodorant and drugs to increase virility and prowess. And in this context, he created opportunities for the talents of scientists, university professors, and planners, whom Arab regimes take pains to train by the hundreds, but then prevent them from using their abilities, so that neither they nor their nations profit.

"Nevertheless, there is another aspect to the subject. I hope you will be magnanimous enough to hear me out. The Doctor attracted me as a subject. He led me into multiple disciplines. On one hand, this would reveal to you my diverse talents, and on the other, impart to the study itself a dimension that would enrich and enhance its importance to the utmost.

"I was thinking about that very point when you honored me with a visit. I determined that the traditional approach, which entails compiling a biography of a person, must be replaced by an innovative method drawing on a number of studies in various scholarly disciplines.

"The first important branch is in the discipline of aesthetics, dealing with extreme patriotism and the uprooting of trees, which in turn connects with a branch of economics concerning the role of buying and selling in the life of nations and individuals. A third branch, within ethics, treats the obsolescence of truth, trust, and honor. Fourth, there is a division of psychology that investigates the roots of the anxiety that motivates geniuses and pioneers to transfer their energies from one field to another. This study might lead to an important discovery about the Doctor's childhood and how he was breast-fed.

"The fifth field of study, within politics and administration, discusses the molding of public opinion into unified mass beliefs and tastes, which can easily be manipulated at will.

"Indeed it gives me great pleasure to announce, with all due pride, that I've come across some unknown but elegant odes composed by him, plus some scattered allusions to his opinions on film, music, and the theater, all in all a suitable basis for a creative study on contemporary literature and art.

"Connected with this is an independent investigation on the development that occurred in the Arabic language. This development finds expression in the disappearance of specific words and the appearance of new ones, some of them unique, unprecedented forms, such as 'pilfer' and 'pretend not to hear,' whereas others, such as 'diversification' and 'naturalization' and 'activization' are newly created derivations of familiar words.

"The Doctor's unique mental flexibility and his capacity for reshaping his attitudes and consistently landing on his feet inspired me to do a study on the psychology of child rearing and character development. Because of the special importance of this study, I hope you will allow me to digress on this point in order to present an example that comes to mind. It stems from the facts presented at the first interview with which I was honored at your headquarters. By that I mean my detailed presentation on Coca-Cola.

"As you have learned, your honors, this bottle entered our country at the end of the '40s and beginning of the '50s under the aegis of the vast advertising campaign that facilitated its spread to even the most remote villages and hamlets. Coca-Cola became a household word.

"After the revolution, Coca-Cola's popularity soon began to wane. I found out that the Doctor, among other factors, was responsible. To wit, he tried to compete by using a local beverage destined to succeed only for a short while.

"However, the crushing blow fell at the beginning of the '60s, when the Arab governmental agencies boycotting Israel discovered that Coca-Cola had given the Israelis bottling rights. As a result, Coca-Cola was blacklisted and barred from Arab countries. The market was wide open for the Doctor.

"As you know, nothing stays the same for long. The Doctor's plan failed for several reasons, which there is no point in enumerating now. The aforementioned boycott necessarily fell apart overnight and furthermore, the Doctor was in the right place at the right time. He got a head start through his efforts to remove the obstacles and obstructions long separating this refreshing drink from its Egyptian aficionados, and as a reward for his efforts, the company granted him bottling rights using a national bottle.

"Perhaps you agree with me, your honors, that this action on the part of Coca-Cola is equivalent in a way to an outright testimony to the Doctor's credit, especially given the fact the mother company only gives this concession to the most luminous person in each country.

"Please bear with me, as this point reminds me of another far-reaching phenomenon which the Doctor's biography will introduce to the ambitious scholar. I mean his sexual life, which is characterized by an extraordinary energy. Such energy might have several widely varying aspects, ranging from excessive virility—the causes of which can be studied to define them and make them available to all—to a continuous attempt to deny latent homosexual tendencies, or the unflagging search for a mother figure, which search clearly manifests itself in his economic dealings as a continual restlessness and an indiscriminate desire to belong."

My throat had dried out. I stopped talking and looked at their faces to determine the effect of my speech. However, they were thickly blanketed in apathy.

I licked my lips, gathered my strength for a final attempt, and hurriedly said, "I would like to speak frankly, your honors, on something else of special importance. The study I have undertaken made me aware of a number of hidden relationships and connections among a collection of strange and diverse phenomena. I believe that very soon I will be able to offer a solution to some of the mysteries and puzzles that have baffled most people until now."

They suddenly showed some interest. I added in a voice that I tried to make as gracious and courteous as possible, "I am confident that out of the goodness of your hearts, you will let me finish what I have begun."

"We won't force you to do anything. You are free to do as you like," the Blond said sharply.

He looked at his watch, thought deeply, and added, "We'll leave now. We can't stay longer. Our comrade," and here he indicated Stubby, "will stay with you until you reach a decision."

He reached out and took the picture of President Carter. Stubby gathered up the index cards with the notes on the American article plus the original notebook I had worked from and handed them to the Blond, who took them in silence. I didn't dare object.

The Blond headed for the bedroom door and everyone else followed. Meanwhile, Stubby remained sitting at my table. When I made to accompany them, he signaled me to stay in my place.

"I'm afraid they'll stumble in the dark. The stairs aren't lit, as you may have noticed. I could help with an electric flashlight," I objected.

He answered me insolently, "They have flashlights and don't need your help."

I listened to their footsteps on the stairs and the noise

of the outer door when the last person closed it behind himself. Meanwhile, I was looking at the ugly face that remained with me. I suddenly realized that I had ended up under his thumb.

But at the same time I felt that the coming ordeal, on which my fate depends, would also be the climax of his.

F ⊙ U R

I sat down on the edge of the bed, lit a cigarette with trembling fingers, and tried to take in the latest turn of events. Above all, I wanted to understand the new situation. I said to Stubby, who hadn't left his place at the table, "I was honored to welcome you, you and the rest of the Committee members to my apartment. However, there is something I'd like to be sure of. To be specific, reaching a decision in this matter will take some time . . ."

"Take however much time you want. What ultimately counts is that you reach a decision."

"It might require a number of days," I said very suavely.

"You must get it into your head that I will stay here until this thing is wrapped up, even if it takes more than a year. Naturally, the sooner the better for you," he said firmly.

Silence fell briefly while I examined his words and their significance. He resumed speaking, "I have no right to stick my nose in this business of your decision, but I am personally in a position to help you."

"Thank you for your generosity. As long as you're offering to help, what do you propose?"

"We suggested you substitute another personality. The Committee will not oppose any alternative whatsoever. Perhaps you could find a suitable format that would allow you to continue along the same lines."

I saw a glimmer of hope. "That's fine with me. So how shall I do it?"

"That's up to you. Think," he answered, and I sensed a touch of sadistic satisfaction.

I couldn't think, although I gave it the old college try. My throat got drier, so I swallowed several times. Finally I suggested we drink some tea.

"If tea will help you think, I've nothing against it," he said snidely.

I got up right away and left the room. He left his seat and followed me. With him behind me, I went down the hall until I reached the kitchen. He stopped in the doorway, watching me. I filled the tea kettle from the tap, put it on the stove, and lit the gas.

I didn't grasp the situation completely until I had to take a leak. I left the kitchen and retraced my steps back along the hall toward the bathroom, which was next to the bedroom. I had no sooner gone into the bathroom and turned to close the door than I found that he had followed me and pushed the door all the way open. He stood in the doorway, near me, until I'd finished my business.

"Did you think I would run away from you?" I said, stepping up to the sink and turning on the tap.

"What I believe is none of your business," he answered insolently.

I washed my hands and face, dried them, then went back to the kitchen with him at my heels.

I made the tea and poured it out, then handed him his cup and picked up mine. I automatically preceded him to the bedroom.

I saw him heading for my seat, so I pulled him up short by saying, "I would like to ask a favor of you."

"What is it?" he said cautiously.

"That you sit in this seat and leave me my place at the table." He looked at me a moment, then his gaze wandered over the room, until it settled on the armchair. He examined it carefully as though looking for some hidden meaning in the request, or some dirty trick. Finally he shrugged his shoulders and said, "It doesn't matter to me."

I occupied my favorite place at the table, my back to the final wall of my apartment and the door in front of me. I didn't ordinarily have any peace except in this position.

Since the armchair was near the door, between it and the bed, Stubby was eyeball to eyeball with me. This made me instantly regret trying so hard for an illusory sense of security.

I offered him a cigarette, but he said he didn't smoke so as not to damage his health. I hurriedly lit my cigarette, fearing he would make me comply with his way of thinking. But he was engaged in contemplating the picture of a naked woman hanging above my head.

I commented on his interest, "It's a Mahmoud Saeed, as perhaps you guessed. Its beauty surpasses its magnificent colors and balanced composition. Perhaps you also noticed the vagueness of the gaze and the position of the hands. In my opinion, it could be compared with the famous Mona Lisa."

For the first time a twisted smile appeared on his face. I was surprised when he winked one eye at me and said, "Have you other pictures of this type?"

"I understand what you're getting at. Unfortunately,

I'm not overly fond of girly pictures. I prefer reading pornography. I have a collection of such books if you'd like to see them."

"Later," he said. "It seems we'll have plenty of time. However, I don't understand why you object to pinups."

"Because they only portray a static moment which has no depth. A book, on the other hand, sheds some light on human behavior. No matter what levels of vulgarity or excesses of imagination the writer descends to, still he is compelled to draw on real experience, and willy-nilly he reveals a side of the human subconscious through what he discloses of his own. The final result may be a source of knowledge, just as much, of course, as it surely is a source of pleasure."

Apparently he had no desire to continue the discussion, and so concentrated on slurping his tea. His gaze shifted between the books and the recordings that filled the several shelves hanging behind me. I took this as an opportunity to organize the ideas raging in my brain.

I was appalled at the thought of starting over on the study, even assuming I could find a personality to replace the Doctor. This personality would have to have an abundance of those qualities that make the Doctor the most luminous contemporary Arab personality and at the same time excite my interest and passion. And who's to say that if I came across another personality, the

Committee wouldn't visit me some months later to demand I replace it again?

My devotion to the Doctor amazed me. It was as though his personality had bewitched me, or as though my existence had become linked to his. Bringing all my thoughts to bear, I saw that I had finally found a meaning in life. It had grown out of the cryptic phenomena which had discouraged me during my research, and out of the strange information I had collected. All my gleanings made it easy for me to perceive many things I had not understood before. I wasn't prepared to give up and return to that aching emptiness in which I had been living. Would a drowning man let go of a life preserver? There was nothing for it but to confine myself to the line of thought my guest had just hinted at.

There was a significance to his proposal and to all the recent developments which did not escape me. The freedom of movement and maneuver granted me up to now, which had enabled me to avoid the growing web of constraints, had decreased to the point of disappearing completely.

This idea annoyed me to the point where I couldn't think anymore. I decided to put it all off until morning, it being my custom to seek refuge in sleep.

"It's late and maybe you'd like a bite to eat," I said to Stubby after a bit.

"Not at all. I ate dinner before I came. You go ahead, if you like."

"I'm worn out. I'm not really hungry and I'd like to get to bed now. Where would you like me to make up your bed?"

"Isn't this your bed?" he asked in turn, indicating the bed.

"Yes," I answered, "I can make you up another bed in the hall. Or you can sleep here and I'll sleep in the hall."

"Neither," he said decisively. "I'm going to sleep next to you in your bed." This really set me on edge. I hadn't forgotten what had happened to me at my first interview with the Committee. Sizing him up, I found him strong as a pile driver in spite of his age. I realized I was no match for him and shouldn't tangle with him.

I discovered he'd brought a Samsonite suitcase along. He now opened it, taking out a leather toiletry case, a towel, and cloth slippers. I watched until he closed it, in case I could catch a glimpse of the contents. He waited until he saw me head for the bathroom, then draped his towel over his shoulder and followed.

While I was brushing my teeth, he took a toothbrush, toothpaste, and perfumed French soap out of his leather case. I quickly finished washing up, then left him the sink. I took this opportunity to pee. Next, I filled some plastic containers from the bath tub tap.

Only at night is there sufficient water pressure to supply the top floors, so I always have to collect enough water to last through the next day.

I explained all this to Stubby when he asked me what I was doing. I left him standing in the doorway while I filled several containers. He noticed that as the container filled, the tap water soon turned a mud color, then black. This was normal in my experience, but he expressed surprise, saying that he had never seen tap water that color.

"You must use a water filter," I said.

"Yes, how did you know?" he said in amazement.

Turning the tap off after filling the last container, I smiled, "I have learned many things recently."

I went to the kitchen with him at my heels. I filled several bottles and containers with water for drinking and cooking and shut the gas off tightly. On the verge of making my nightly rounds to close the windows and lock the front door, I stopped short, since it was evident that what I feared, tonight at least, wasn't outside.

We finally returned to the bedroom. He took embroidered silk pajamas out of his suitcase. I suggested that he change in the bathroom, or that I leave the room until he'd finished. Naturally, he didn't agree. I didn't really care, since it wouldn't embarrass me to be naked in front of a man like him. All the more so since this fellow already had knowledge of the most intimate parts of my body.

Having taken off my outer clothes, I stood before him in my underwear. I felt awkward whenever he looked at me. I couldn't resist glancing at his naked thighs. The bulge of what was between them scared me. I supposed that either he was the victim of an old hernia, so that his guts were taking liberties with his testicles, or that he was created with unusual generosity.

I wanted to raise the question of sleeping arrangements again. I said, suddenly animated, "Perhaps you'd like to read a little before going to sleep. In that case, we'd have to sleep in separate rooms, because light disturbs me and I want to get to sleep right away."

"Don't worry," he said calmly. "I won't read anything. I also want to get right to sleep."

I approached the bed reluctantly. I heard him ask me in the same calm voice to get into bed first so that he could sleep on the outer edge.

I acceded to his request and lay down on my back next to the wall. He joined me as soon as he put out the light.

Needless to say, I couldn't get the sleep I so badly needed. I had to wake up the next morning refreshed and capable of sorting out the dilemma confronting me. Although I desperately needed to sleep after an arduous day, my ignorance of how far my bedmate would go stimulated all my senses, especially my ears.

At first, the thump of my rapid heart beats drowned out the familiar night sounds. When I calmed down a little, I noticed the pipes rattling, the clamor of the neighbor's children, water splashing into a metal tub in the apartment below mine, and dogs barking in the neighborhood streets.

The strange thing was that these noises, which had so often enraged me and deprived me of sleep, were a source of peace that night, soothing the tension in my nerves.

However, I started when gunshots resounded through the still night in declaration of open season on the dogs.

I knew most of these dogs. Days, I'd see their emaciated bodies in the local streets and on garbage heaps. They were cowards, all bark and no bite. The most they dared do was raise their voices at inopportune times, especially after people retired for the night.

Apparently the barking reverberating through the stillness of the night had hurt the ears of some luminary among the neighbors. So, he hired someone to hunt the dogs down. On most nights, the barking began to be mingled with gunfire until eventually it disappeared.

The following day or the next the barking would return to its previous intensity as though nothing had happened. Then the gunfire would resound again.

My bedmate paid no attention to the gunfire, continuing to lie quietly on his back. I held my breath when he suddenly turned onto his left side to face me.

His perfumed scent wafted over to me, gagging me. Presently, from the regularity of his breathing I concluded that he was sound asleep. I turned onto my right side facing him. In the dark, I looked toward his face.

Since I had gotten used to the dark, I could see his eyes. It startled me that they were open, staring vigilantly.

I closed my eyes at once and pretended to sleep, but watched him from under half-closed eyelids.

Suddenly his hand moved. Scared, I held my breath. I had got it into my head that he would touch me. But he didn't, and his breathing remained regular. It seemed to me he'd closed his eyes, but I didn't trust my imagination. Perhaps, like me, he was watching through his eyelashes.

It was difficult for me to sleep with the problems on my mind. Whenever I tried thinking of something else, I would open the Pandora's box I had been trying to lock. Images and memories that had been waiting popped right into my head. Immediately my weaknesses and flaws stood out plainly. My emotions ran wild at the thought of my insignificance, of the moments when I had permitted myself to be the laughing-stock of others and a plaything in their hands, of how I allowed myself to be sidetracked, and of the small pleasures I had indulged in and allowed to dominate me.

No sooner had I become uncertain about these very matters, than a familiar wave of doubt swamped me, casting its shadows over my life's aims and goals. Nor were the sexual pleasures that occupied a conspicuous place in my emotional life left untouched. In a desperate attempt to save myself, I called upon the memories and fantasies my mind had stored up, which had never yet failed to stir the blood in my veins. Nevertheless, I found myself unresponsive, numb to every promise of pleasure.

Near dawn I must have dozed a little and turned my back to him. I was suddenly alerted by something firm bumping my thigh. I stiffened onto my back at once. I looked toward him and in the thin dawn light I saw him staring watchfully at me. But he was far enough away to make me believe I'd been dreaming. You can see what was running through my mind.

Naturally I couldn't sleep after that. When the sun's rays shone in, I decided to get up. He preceded me, and we got out of bed together. We went along to the bathroom, took a leak, and washed up.

I saw him take his razor out of the leather case. I decided to shave too, hoping to clear my mind and keep busy until he finished. I was sure he wouldn't let me leave the bathroom any earlier.

We stood together in front of the mirror over the sink. I raised my red, watery eyes. They met his, which were full of vitality and energy, as though he had enjoyed a full night's sleep. A steady gaze met mine, which I was at a loss to explain since he was walleyed. The razor shook in my hand, nicking me under the chin.

Unable to stand the sight of blood or the thought of pain, I began to shake all over. I saw myself staring at the trickle of blood oozing from the wound, with a certain feeling of curiosity.

My companion snapped me out of my trance when, from the leather case, he handed me a small bottle of scented liquid with which to treat the cut. I declined politely and stuck my whole head under the tap, letting the thin stream of water wash the wound and staunch it.

After I had dried my head and stuck a small piece of cotton on the cut, we went back to the bedroom to change our clothes. I contented myself with pants and a shirt. He put on a complete suit, right down to the necktie.

We went to the kitchen and I made tea. There were only three eggs in the fridge. After asking my guest's preference, I put them on the stove in a little water. I also took out a piece of cheese, another of sesame halva, and some black olives.

We finally sat down facing each other across the dining table. I offered him two boiled eggs out of the three and conferred the third on myself. He didn't comment on this unequal apportionment, but instead applied himself to his food with great relish, whereas I just picked at mine.

We soon finished eating. I poured the tea. My newspapers came, delivered by the vendor as usual to the front doorstep. I gave Stubby one and kept the other.

Lately I had developed the habit of combining four activities: drinking tea, smoking my first cigarette, reading the daily paper, and attending to a bodily need. I'd gotten into this habit when I began my research on the Doctor. I had had to cut down the time between getting up and leaving my apartment in order to spend as much time as possible at the publishing houses of the newspapers and magazines whose libraries I haunted. However, this custom was rooted in an instinctive sense of the appropriate place to read our national newspapers. Like all habits, it came to be a cornerstone of my daily mental routine. Whenever I relinquished it or deviated from it even slightly, my whole day was ruined right from the start.

I didn't feel there was anything preventing me from

following my routine that day, especially since I was in more need than ever of all my mental faculties, as well as of whatever time alone I could get. I put my pack of cigarettes and my matches in my pocket, tucked the paper under my arm, picked up my cup, and went along to the bathroom.

I expected him to follow me like always, and so he did. I set my cup on the edge of the sink and confronted him, explaining what I had in mind and how it was contingent on closing the door.

He looked at me derisively, "Have you forgotten I saw your bare backside under conditions less dignified than answering a call of nature?"

"I haven't forgotten. But it's customary for a person to tend to this business by himself. This is a very private moment."

He said maliciously, "If you must wave other peoples' dirty laundry in public, can you expect to wash your own in private?"

Having determined the attempt was futile, I pulled down my pants and sat on the plastic toilet seat. He stood in the doorway watching me.

I picked up my teacup, took a couple of sips, then put it on the floor by my feet. I took out a cigarette and lit it. Then I unfolded the paper and began with the headlines.

But the usual harmony of the morning didn't develop. Neither the tea nor the cigarette had any flavor and I couldn't concentrate on reading. More important than all that, my bowels wouldn't move.

I had no hope of making any progress by staying in this position. I got up, pulled my pants up quickly, and headed for the bedroom, feeling deeply depressed and frustrated. I sat at my desk while he occupied the armchair.

I lit a new cigarette and reached for the index cards filed in the shoebox. Feeling Stubby's gaze on my face, I began leafing through them.

I had to find some method that would satisfy and be sanctioned by the Committee so I could continue the research I had begun. Could this be done by eliminating certain parts of his biography? Or by restricting my approach to a single aspect of his rich personality? And what would that aspect be? Or should I completely abandon the novel program I had proposed to the Committee and instead employ a traditional biographical format?

The harder I thought the more hopeless I felt. The traditional format was fraught with the grave dangers I had alluded to at the time. On the other hand, it made the connections between aspects of his career and personality clear, so much so that it would be difficult to deal with the two separately.

How is it possible to speak of wealth without alluding to its source? And too, if I ignored the related facts, I would violate the basic principle that Balzac crystalized in his celebrated maxim: "Behind every great fortune is a great crime," which has since become a premise of all modern researchers.

Likewise, it was not possible for me to disregard his humble origin, or his patriotic role and connections with the revolution, or his appeal for Arab unity, socialism, or his diverse economic activities, or his brokering for foreign companies and the international awards he won for this, or his greed for the Gulf petroleum wealth, which goes to its real owners in Europe and the United States via other middlemen. What would be left of him if I did?

Stubby suddenly addressed me in a friendly manner, seemingly uninterested, "Incidentally, yesterday I heard you speak about the important discoveries you had arrived at in your studies on the Doctor. If my memory doesn't fail me, you said you could tear the veil from many mysteries. What did you mean?"

I sensed danger and tried to avoid answering.

I said nonchalantly, "In fact, I haven't yet come up with anything. What I meant to say, and perhaps I didn't express myself accurately, is that I'm on the brink of understanding the relationships between a number of miscellaneous phenomena."

"Such as?"

I thought a bit, then said, "The phenomena are many, innumerable, so that it is difficult to choose only one of them. Take, for example, the spread of the maladies of mental depression, sexual impotence, apathy, religious fanaticism, the extinction of the Egyptian cigarette, or the return of Coca-Cola. Wherever you look you will find the phenomenon you want."

I smiled and added, "Indeed, the Doctor himself provides us with one of the most provocative and inexplicable phenomena. By that I mean the presence of many like him in each Arab nation, in spite of disparate social and political systems, characteristics, and laws."

He ignored my reference to the Doctor and shook his head scornfully, "And where is this alleged relationship between the phenomena?"

Cunningly, I answered, "I didn't say I'd discovered it. I'm only beginning my research."

Enunciating every syllable, he said emphatically, "I see you're chasing a mirage, imagining something that doesn't exist, for how does an ordinary study like the one you're doing lead up to all these matters?"

I banged the desktop and said, "This is what I constantly keep repeating to myself to no avail . . . What would you think about a cup of coffee?"

He was surprised at the change of subject, but quickly said, "I have no objection."

Then he looked at his watch and corrected himself, "Better if I don't. It's nearly dinnertime."

I got up and said brightly, "Unfortunately I wasn't expecting this visit, so I didn't prepare for it. Actually, I have enough rice, but as for the fridge . . . Well, I believe there's at least half a chicken, but then again one has to fix some side dishes. Something like soup and some kind of meat or fish dish, another of vegetables, to say nothing of fruit and desert. Thus, you see, I have to go—I mean—we have to go to the market."

He said, propelling me toward the kitchen, "Don't bother. We'll make do with what you have on hand."

I shrugged my shoulders as if to absolve myself of responsibility, took the half chicken out of the freezer, and put it in some water to thaw. I lit a burner under a pan of water, cleaned the chaff out of the rice, and poured the hot water over it, reserving enough for the cup of coffee I so badly needed.

I washed the rice thoroughly in hot water and transferred it to another pan. I added butter, salt, and a little liquid, then put it back on the heat. Going back to the fridge, I took out tomatoes, cucumbers, and green peppers, then opened the utensil drawer located under the burner to look for a clean knife. I only found a large, sharp butcher knife. I closed the drawer on it and took a couple of sips of coffee. My companion stood in the doorway of the kitchen, dividing his attention between keeping an eye on me and scanning the titles of the books arranged in rows running from the kitchen to the bathroom. I asked him to pour me some water so I could wash the paring knife.

As he poured, he indicated the nearest pile of books, "You like detective stories?"

"Definitely."

"But I see that you don't have even one work by Agatha Christie."

Drying the knife and hurriedly chopping the vegetables, I replied, "I only like certain kinds of detective stories: those based on action. The ones I like best have a hero who pursues criminals and gangsters and suffers every hardship in the process. Most of the time he protects the weak or defenseless from society and the dominant classes."

"You're a real humanitarian," he said derisively.

Sipping my coffee, I said, "Not at all. Indeed, some people might think I'd regressed to adolescence. Others might consider it merely evidence of the child within every person. But I believe there's more to it than that.

Our fascination with this kind of story expresses an inability to act when necessary and goes hand in hand
with the natural, rightful desire of every person for evil
to be punished and good to triumph."

After a moment, I continued, "Such stories don't require much mental effort from the reader, because they
are built on action. However, this doesn't mean that
Agatha Christie's stories are distinguished by a high
intellectual level. From a flight of fancy, she creates
simplistic mysteries not worth puzzling over when reality itself teems with true mysteries requiring all one's
faculties."

Trying to get under my skin, he said, "Now we're
getting back to discussing unsolved mysteries and
strange phenomena. I'm beginning to wonder whether
you're of sound mind."

I understood that he was pulling my leg, but I didn't
rise to the bait, rather waved the knife in the direction
of the tap and said, "You're laughing at me. But what
about the black tap water? Isn't that a true mystery?"

"And what else?" he said calmly.

I plunged ahead rashly, "There are many of them, if
you like, take the Doctor's position on the problem of
war and peace. In some short newspaper interviews, he
portrayed war as the only means for recovery of usurped

rights. Meanwhile, in other interviews he asserted that peace was the only means."

He interrupted me to ask, "What's the inconsistency?"

"The inconsistency is that in the first case, when he speaks of war, you find him working energetically on projects that require, indeed require first and foremost, peace. In the second case, when he speaks of peace, you find him caught up in forming a corps of mercenaries to offer to whomever will pay the price."

I stopped to check the rice and turn down the burner. Then I rinsed the half chicken and readied a frying pan.

I continued, "If these aren't enough, there is a third mystery for you. The instructions on foreign medicines sold in our country prescribe a larger dosage than that prescribed for patients in the countries where they are manufactured. Why?"

I put two tablespoons of oil in the frying pan and slid the half chicken in, having stepped back a little so that the hot oil wouldn't spatter me.

Still at the height of enthusiasm, I said, "How do you account for the map hanging in the Israeli Knesset? Although the Israelis proclaim that it was their ancestors who built the pyramids located on the western bank of the Nile, this map shows Israel's proposed borders on the eastern bank."

He didn't bother to argue, being more interested in listening, as though giving me enough rope to hang myself. I noticed this suddenly, when a gleam of enjoyment appeared in one of his eyes. Putting the food on the table gave me the opportunity to change the subject.

Sitting down opposite him, I said, "Perhaps you noticed my collection of stories by the Belgian writer Georges Simenon. I am truly a devotee of him and his hero, Inspector Maigret. Although his stories are not 'action oriented,' being closer to true mystery stories, they nevertheless surpass Agatha Christie's in that they are distinctive for their psychological depth and sociological dimension. They substantiate the fact that most of an ordinary man's contradictory attitudes are stored up in the unconscious. At a certain point in this accumulation, something occurs, like the straw that broke the camel's back, and the man acts completely out of character with everything he has ever done. A peaceful man who has never committed a single violent act is capable of perpetrating the most heinous crime of premeditated murder."

He didn't comment, but gave himself up wholeheartedly to eating with his familiar appetite. I began to watch him quietly. He clutched the drumstick firmly, carried it to his mouth with a steady hand, then bit into it with gusto. Concentrating hard, he chewed until it was pulverized.

It occurred to me what was missing in my life—to be precise, this manner of eating, which springs from an interest in life, a lack of hesitation in meeting danger, and persistence in defeating it.

We finished eating. I cleared away the dishes and put them in the kitchen sink. We went along to the bathroom and washed up. After that, we holed up in the inner room, each settling into his place.

I lit a cigarette. No sooner had I taken two puffs than the familiar drowsiness I always feel after eating overcame me. I felt that my exertions had stretched me to my limits and that I was in dire need of a short nap.

"Wouldn't you like a bit of a rest? I usually sleep a little after dinner," I remarked.

He took his time answering. "It isn't my custom to sleep during the day. And as for you, I don't believe you're in a position to waste time sleeping."

I understood what he meant and turned my attention to the box of index cards. I began to leaf through them, although my burning eyes couldn't make out anything written on them.

He'd relaxed peacefully in his chair, his eyes fixed on the ceiling, on a point above my head. He became completely absorbed in his thoughts. It was as if he'd turned into a statue.

My head felt heavy, so I let it droop forward a little. I couldn't resist the temptation to close my eyes. Suddenly, he addressed me urgently, "Could you accompany me for a moment?"

I saw that he had stood up tensely. Startled, I left my seat. My heart began to pound. I followed him out. He went into the bathroom saying, "Please stay right there until I'm done."

He left the door open so he could see me. After dropping his pants, he settled onto the plastic seat. I turned my back and stood looking at the books arranged along the hall, most of which I had purchased in preparation for my first interview with the Committee. I had arranged them strictly by subject, grouping the economic and political studies together, including some excellent studies on foreign interests in the Arab world and a distinguished work on the military in third-world countries. The latter study included a brilliant chapter on the roots of the obviously sadistic behavior of third-world leaders, which may shed some light on the bloodthirstiness of Arab leaders.

I had reserved a corner for the most important works of serious literature. Many names were ranged there, from Shakespeare, Pushkin, and Cervantes to Garcia Marquez and Naguib Mahfouz.

In a prominent place I collected everything pertinent to the careers of several world figures, such as the prophet Muhammad, Abu Dharr al-Ghafari, Abu Sa'id al-Jinabi, Ibn Rushd, al-Ma'arri, Karl Marx, Freud, Lenin, Jamal al-Din al-Afghani, Taha Husayn, Madam Curie, Albert Schweitzer, Fucik, Castro, Guevarra, Lumumba, Ibn Baraka, Shohdi Attia, and Gamal Abd al-Nasser, who set the standards for human endeavor by their ideas, experiences, and sacrifices.

A sharp metallic sound roused me from my contemplation of these names. In spite of myself, I turned around to see a strange sight: his pants bunched around his ankles and the rest of his body bare, Stubby was leaning over to pick up a big black revolver that had fallen to the floor.

He lifted the revolver with a quick movement and lodged it between his thighs, then pulled up his trousers. He stole a glance in my direction. But I had turned away from him just in time.

I understood—and my heart beat violently—the secret of that bulge I had previously noticed between his thighs. This meant that I hadn't been dreaming this morning when I imagined something firm bumping my thigh. I almost smiled when I saw that out of fear I had reversed the well-known Freudian axiom in which a gun is a symbol for the penis.

No sooner had the humor of the situation faded than a feeling of danger seized me again. This feeling stuck with me as we returned to the bedroom and took our places opposite each other.

Suddenly something occurred to me that made me hold my breath—what if I were to refuse?

What would he say if I revealed I wasn't willing to abandon my research or change the subject? What if I were determined to finish it, bringing it to its natural conclusion, and to accept whatever that would do to my chances with the Committee?

I found that this idea relieved me greatly. It was as though it lifted a great burden from my shoulders. I looked at him, considering the situation. It seemed to me that he grasped the drift of my thoughts, because he suddenly smiled derisively.

This smile unnerved me and made me wonder. Could this really be so simple? You are free to accept or refuse. If you refuse, he would say, "Fine. That's your business. I'll leave you now. I don't think we'll meet again. Farewell." Then you would accompany him to the front door saying, "Goodbye and good luck." And that would be the end of it.

Then why does he need the revolver?

For the first time, I fully realized the delicacy of my position. I lit a fresh cigarette and tried to control the trembling of my hand.

I closed my eyes and reviewed my past. The ideals I had believed in while growing up surfaced. I had gradually eliminated those that were clearly naïve and unrealistic, although I had tried desperately not to give them up, and I had kept those that were important and valuable, plus those consistent with my nature and abilities. Indeed, feeling torn, I had struggled to reevaluate them every so often and to develop them to accommodate the continual changes in the modern world, avoiding as many pitfalls and labyrinths as possible, although throughout all this I was exposed to a great deal of harm and innumerable dangers.

I thought back over where my life had been heading before the Committee interviewed me and how I suffered humiliation at its "hand." However, I didn't forget that the assigned research had given some meaning to my life after a long spell of hopelessness.

I opened my eyes to find him looking at me.

I laughed, hoping it would be infectious, and said in a voice I tried to keep normal, "How about a cup of coffee? I absolutely can't keep my eyes open."

"As you like."

We went to the kitchen. I looked at the small mirror hanging in the hall and saw that my eyes were bloodshot.

When we reached the kitchen I asked him, "Have you any objection to drinking Turkish coffee this time?"

He didn't reply; he was busy checking the contents of the "Hall Library" as I called it. I interpreted his last response as acceptance.

I took the medium-sized coffeepot from one of the shelves and asked him again, "How do you prefer yours?"

"Not too much sugar."

He picked up the closest book and began to turn its pages with one eye still on me. I couldn't find a small spoon on the drain board, so I opened the utensil drawer. My eyes went right to the butcher knife, that large, shiny blade with a tapered tip.

My heart leaped between my ribs. I got ahold of myself and took the spoon that I wanted, then closed the drawer.

I put the coffee and sugar in the pot, filled it with water, stirred the mixture well, and put it on the small burner I had lit.

I washed the spoon and dried it, then opened the drawer and set the spoon by the knife, looking at its sharp edge. Without taking my eyes off the knife, I pushed the drawer in slowly, deliberately leaving it ajar.

I stood in front of the coffeepot until it began to bub-
ble and then foam up as it came to a boil. It surged
higher until it almost overflowed the rim.

I quickly removed it from the heat and turned off the
burner. I put two cups beside it.

For the first time in ages, I felt strength and purpose
pervade my being.

- Radothun
- Revolting to the oppression of every
  exploitive structure.

F İ V E

This time when I arrived for my appointment, the Committee had already gathered. The old porter admitted me at once.

I found its members, naturally except for Stubby, seated behind a long table set crosswise in the hall. They were in the same order I had seen the previous time, with the decrepit old man who couldn't see or hear in the middle.

I noted the unmitigated atmosphere of mourning evidenced by the black ribbons on their jacket collars and the floral wreaths arranged at one side of the room, each wrapped with shiny black cloth. Also attached to each was a memorial placard with the name of the sender in prominent letters.

The members of the Committee began to eye me, though still examining the files in front of them. Mean-

while, curious, I read the names of the mourners. Right
in front I discovered the names of the American president Carter and his wife, the first lady, his vice president, Walter Mondale, and his national security advisor,
Brzezinski. I also saw the names of his predecessor,
Kissinger, and several former American presidents such
as Nixon and Ford, as well as of Rockefeller, Rothschild,
MacNamara (president of the World Bank), the president of Coca-Cola, directors of international banks,
presidents of companies that manufacture weapons,
chewing gum, drugs, cigarettes, electronics, and petroleum, and in addition, the leaders of France, West Ger-
many, England, Italy, Austria, the heads of Mercedes,
Peugeot, Fiat, Bedford, Boeing, and the emperor of
Japan.

I easily found the names of the Israeli prime minister,
Begin, and his ministers Dayan and Weizman; and the
presidents of the military governments of Chile, Turkey,
Pakistan, Indonesia, the Philippines, and Bolivia; and of
Mubutu (the president of Zaire), and of Arab kings and
presidents; members of the former shah of Iran's family;
Mama Doc (the first lady of Haiti); the presidents of
Communist China and Romania, of both North and
South Korea, and the leaders of the Australian people.

The names of many luminaries from the Arab world
were there: directors of leading political parties, senior

officials in charge of security, information, defense, planning, and construction, the authorized agents of foreign companies, not to mention the more luminous "doctors," among them my well-known countryman.

When I finally turned my attention to the Committee members, I sensed that since the last time I had seen them they had undergone some change I couldn't put my finger on. This aroused my curiosity further. I looked them over, searching for some explanation. Their scowling faces weren't new to me. In spite of the dark glasses most of them wore, I recognized the same individuals I had met twice before.

Unable to think, for a third time I failed to count them. Nevertheless I was certain their number hadn't changed, except, of course, for Stubby. His place next to the old man was empty. It was swathed in black, like his picture, which hung on the wall as a reminder of his demise.

I solved the mystery only after looking at the old maid several times. When I noticed she was wearing a military uniform with red ribbons edged in gold, I finally realized what I had been oblivious to from the beginning.

Perhaps I was so slow to figure this out because I was accustomed to seeing three officers among the Committee members. This number had registered in my unconscious from the first moment. I was content with it and didn't pay attention to their identities. To me, they all looked alike because of the uniforms.

Now I looked closely at the other officers to determine their sex and identities. I searched for the third until, with difficulty, I found him. Wearing civilian clothes had greatly altered his appearance.

This phenomenon really piqued my curiosity. Having been trained by the events of the last year to solve mysteries and riddles, my mind raced, trying to come up with an explanation.

Formerly, I had believed the Committee was a combination of civilians and officers. But, as I had seen today, the change in dress shook this belief to its foundations. It could mean only one of two things: the Committee consists entirely of officers, some of whom sometimes wear civilian clothes, or it consists of civilians, some of whom sometimes wear military uniforms.

In neither case was there any significance to the change. Actually, abandoning the uniforms could be considered a weakening of the military streak in the Committee. For a fleeting moment this hope was inviting, in view of the reputation soldiers have for cruelty and bloodthirstiness. That the old maid wore a uniform intensified this hope, since she, by virtue of her femininity (frustrated though it be) was more humane. On the contrary, I soon saw that for this very reason, it was a confirmation rather than a weakening of the military streak.

Using the Committee's language, the chairman snapped me out of my reverie when he said in a sonorous and mournful tone, "Let us begin today by pausing for five minutes to mourn the departed." The members pushed back their chairs and stood. I didn't move because I was already standing. The Committee does not allow anyone to sit in its presence.

I raised my eyes to the picture of the deceased hanging on the wall behind the chairman. I stared into his eyes, in sympathy with the Committee members. While the five minutes crawled by, I tried to concentrate on remembering the way his eyes had moved, each in its own direction, during his full life.

The chairman cleared his throat a number of times, as though he was charging a battery that powered his voice. Then he began to address his colleagues. Looking all the while at the floral wreaths, as though in actuality addressing their senders, he hurriedly said,

"Your honors, respected members. This is one of those exceptional times when the Committee has convened to discuss a matter at variance with its normal experience. This is the third time we have gathered on account of the departed. If my memory serves, the first time was in the mid-50s, when we decided to admit him to the Committee. I still remember him as he was then, full of youth and vitality. The next time was the year before last, when we celebrated his winning the Golden Eagle Prize in recognition of his efforts to serve the Committee's goals.

"Truly, the departed played an important role in devising most of the impressive transformations that have taken place around us and in molding the form in which they materialized.

"The possibility of fulfilling the dreams of mankind and putting an end to all the dangers that threatened the human race is unfolding. They had arisen in the '50s, but were buried in the '60s and early '70s and due to our colleague's role are again springing up.

"Here we refer to that old dream of global unity or a United States of the Earth, in which all the inhabitants of the planet would be incorporated into a homogeneous state fostering prosperity and attempting to provide a better life.

"This underscores the depth of the loss afflicting us. The cause of civilization and progress has suffered, as well as the causes of socialism, peace, and democracy."

He paused a moment to give the others an opportunity to deduce the conclusion he was leading up to, then resumed, "In all our dealings we have been careful to remain disassociated from any direct connection to official bodies and executive authorities, in spite of the rumors that have clung to us and that on several occasions have had a basis in reality. These rumors cast doubt on the aforementioned precept, although, in truth, they confirmed it.

"Now we are faced with a similar situation whose seriousness forces us to attend to it. You well know its implications for the future.

"What compounds the delicacy of the situation is the anguish and distress you are now subjected to, through being directly confronted by the pair of hands stained with the blood of your comrade."

An angry muttering arose among the members, none of whom took their eyes off me even once. I found myself compelled to speak. In contrast to what I expected, my voice came out shaky, using words other than those I had prepared.

"I hope you can find it in your hearts to let me present my side. I am sure you will be so magnanimous and generous as to allow me to speak Arabic in order to better express myself. You may be sure that I share in the pain of your loss, for it is a loss to us all."

The Blond interrupted me angrily, "You will speak when we give you permission."

The old man took a sip of water from the cup in front of him, then continued, "From the beginning the Com-

mittee has put itself at the service of revolutionary ob-
jectives, ethical principles, and religious values. Its
members have supported everything that would
strengthen basic freedoms and expand the democratic
process.

"Naturally, we thus aroused the animosity of evil and
destructive elements, which did their utmost to resist
us. In this connection, let me draw your attention to the
carefully manufactured uproar over the methods we use
in our work and to the charges, sometimes of sadism and
sometimes of demagoguery, that are liberally levied
against us.

"These forces have always tried to link us to political
coups d'état, sectarian massacres, and limited conflicts
happening now in the Arab world, and even to some unexplained suicides, a few sporadic incidents of persons
missing without a trace, and other persons who fell from
rooftops or were killed in chance traffic accidents.

"However, the attack on our comrade represents a
dangerous escalation of these activities, something that
requires your special attention. Your duty might seem
clear because the criminal stands before you and admits
to the heinous crime, but nevertheless, there's more to
this than meets the eye, and your job is to get to the bot-
tom of it."

The old man appeared worn out. He leaned back in

his chair as if to make room for his colleagues. The old maid, now in uniform, was the first to address me,

"You may speak now."

Her voice was gentle, but her allusion to the Blond's response intensified its underlying harshness, since it implied support for his anger.

I'd truly been careful to observe their looks, the way they held their heads, and their tone of voice, in short, all the signs that might predict the fate awaiting me.

This didn't mean I was yielding to despair. Even before I arrived I was prepared for the worst. From the beginning I hadn't denied anything or tried to justify the act. On the other hand, I felt no regret since I was convinced that what had happened was inevitable.

Thus I had prepared my defense as an attack on the Committee. I chose powerful words. Inasmuch as the result was preordained, there was no harm in protecting my dignity and meeting the inevitable with pride and disdain.

However, as soon as I faced the Committee and heard the chairman's words, my resolve vanished. My voice came out shaky and weak, whereas I had intended it to ring firmly through the hall, proud and accusing.

Using the Committee's language, I said, my voice fading away, "Thank you for the opportunity you have granted me to address you. I would like to affirm yet again my awareness of the depth of your loss. It isn't every day the Committee loses one of its members." (I smiled in spite of myself, but they, naturally, did not smile in response.)

"I am telling the truth in saying that when I came today, I did not plan to defend myself. I acknowledge what I did and am willing to face the consequences. Because of this, I am hopeful that my story, my good intentions, and the circumstances will intercede for me.

"I believe you know very well that I have never before committed a violent act. I'm just an ordinary man who prefers as much peace and quiet as possible. The daring acts others speak of and brag about have no connection with me other than as the stuff of stories and novels.

"When I appeared before you the first time, my only goal was to obtain your approval, since I understood it was the only way to develop and demonstrate my talents, especially as the most gifted people had already appeared before you.

"The developments that came afterward were basically due to a desire for knowledge. What I did to your colleague, or to be more accurate, to his chest, was only the natural reaction of a simple person in a situation of self-defense."

The chairman cut me off, "But you stated immediately that he had not attacked you or tried to harm you."

"That's true," I said, "but he carried a revolver. Therefore, from the beginning there was an implied threat of violence. It is certain that if I had not done away with him quickly, he would never have left me in peace. I don't want to defend my position. What I do desire is that you take into consideration the state of my nerves and mind and the fact that I didn't sleep at all while he was with me, not to mention how he dogged my every step."

Staring at me with his merciless light-colored eyes, the Blond leaned toward me and said, "So you want us to buy this picture of a well-intentioned, innocent man you're trying to sell us?"

As I had noticed, he always used—intentionally— the distinctive idioms of the Committee's language. These were expressions which I admired.

I said, "I'm not selling anything, although today anything can be bought and sold, as the study I undertook on the Doctor proved to me. I am simply stating the truth."

He laughed derisively, "Perhaps you think us naïve. You must know that from the first moment you stood before us, we realized that you say one thing and think another. Your answers to the questions we posed were pat and precise, which aroused our suspicions.

"If there was one of us who still wavered, he came to a

decision when you used the assigned study as a pretext for prying into the Doctor's past and for collecting information on him. You insisted on continuing this study in spite of the various warnings sent your way."

He now directed himself to the Committee members, "All the evidence confirms that we are facing a great conspiracy. For some time its threads have been woven very skillfully and maliciously. The attack on the deceased's life is nothing but another thread in the tapestry."

I got very upset at what the Blond said. Matters were moving in a surprising direction that had not occurred to me, and the result could only be extremely damaging to my position.

Laughing and making every attempt to appear innocent and congenial, not to mention ingenuous, I quickly said, "Your honor possesses an active imagination. Surely you don't take what you say seriously?"

He shot back angrily, "Deviousness won't do you any good."

"I assure you I'm innocent."

"Do you also retract your confession?" he asked in reproof.

I replied, "I'm not trying to exonerate myself . . . I'm trying to say there is no plot, or if there is, then I don't know about it."

He said triumphantly, "Aha, so you do acknowledge the existence of a plot."

Frightened, I said, "Never. I only wanted to affirm once again . . ."

The Blond signaled to one of the members seated at the end of the table, who then took out a tape recorder and placed it on top of the table.

The Blond addressed the Committee members, "I will now show you, your honors, how, with his own tongue, he admitted the existence of his accomplices."

The member turned on the tape recorder. I heard a strange noise which I soon identified as water falling onto a hard surface. Then a man spoke, expressing his surprise at the black color of the water. I recognized Stubby's voice and began to tremble.

I heard my voice say, "You must use a water filter."

Stubby's voice followed, surprised, "Yes, how did you know?"

And finally my voice, "I have learned many things recently."

The Blond signaled the operator, who turned the recorder off and addressed me scornfully, "Isn't this your voice?"

"Certainly . . . But that doesn't mean . . ."

He didn't let me continue, but shouted, "How did you come to know this bit of information about our companion that we ourselves didn't know unless you had accomplices who supplied you with information?"

The old maid entered the conversation, "This plot didn't necessarily exist from the beginning. Maybe it was hatched later. His statement that he had learned many things recently indicates this."

She went on to address me, "It would be better for you, because it would mean that your intentions were innocent in the beginning, but that you fell under the influence of deviants, destructive elements. If you tell us their names, it might go a long way toward mitigating the consequences for you."

I wrung my hands hopelessly and said in a voice I tried to make sincere, "Please believe me. Everything happened entirely by chance."

One of the members asked, "Didn't someone provide the knife you used?"

"Absolutely not," I answered, "It was just there—as I stated before—in the kitchen."

Another member asked me, "How did you get to know the things you hinted at?"

"From the newspapers."

The member laughed and looked at his companions as though he did not believe the papers could be a source of information.

I explained, "My research on the Doctor forced me to

consult the issues from a twenty-five-year period. This enabled me to examine facts and events in context and arrive at valuable conclusions which made it easy for me to explain many contemporary phenomena."

One of the officers suddenly leaned forward and said, "Are you going to tell us about these 'phenomena' as you call them?"

Exhausted, I replied, "In view of the sophisticated devices at your disposal, I believe that my answer to this question, which was previously posed by the deceased, is contained in the papers before you."

He leafed through several papers in front of himself and said, "Of course, of course. Here we have um . . . mental illness and the Egyptian cigarette . . . tap water . . . foreign medicines and Coca-Cola. But you haven't explained why you consider these phenomena and these alone worthy of attention."

"I never said that. I cited them as supporting evidence. The phenomena are infinite."

"You also avoided discussing what you discovered about them, as when you hinted at the relationship between them without explaining what you meant by that."

I thought quickly until I reached a decision. Finally recognizing that complete honesty and frankness were the safest means of defense, I said, "I will speak to you openly in order to demonstrate my true intentions and inner feelings. Actually, on one hand, I am the victim of my own ambition, and, on the other, of a passion for knowledge. If it had not been for this latter trait, I would not be in this plight now."

The officer interrupted me, "It would be better to get right to the point."

I said, "I only wanted to explain how I was led to think about these phenomena and to search for an explanation for them. However, as I gathered information, I soon noticed that treating one in isolation would not lead me anywhere. The same result awaited me if, without having a sound method of research, I took them as a unit, because of the mutual relations between them.

"Thus I arrived at a starting point—how to determine a method suitable to explain all the phenomena separately and in relationship to each other."

They pricked up their ears. I understood I had fully aroused their curiosity, so I continued, "I devoted myself to trying out all the familiar approaches without getting anywhere. That very day I was thinking about this when I said to myself, 'The problem with these phenomena and mysteries is that they are not related to just one facet of life, but extend through diverse facets. This means that multiplicity is the common denominator.'

"Here I remembered one of the important conclusions I had arrived at in my research on the Doctor, that is, his participation in the development of the Arabic language by coining new meanings from common words, among them the unique term 'diversification.' In this I found my goal."

The obese member spoke for the first time. He had been wearing a white jacket at my first interview and had now changed it for one of red velvet. He said, "Could you give us an example of what it means?"

I answered, "I was just about to do so. As my example, I will take a subject known to us all, Coca-Cola. Many obscure phenomena are linked to the evolution of this well-known beverage.

"For example, I read of a far-reaching crusade launched in 1970 in the United States over the mistreatment of a quarter million migrant workers on farms controlled by Coca-Cola. I mean farms, not factories. This crusade spread to television and from there to Congress. Senator Walter Mondale, at that time a member of the Committee for Migrant Workers, summoned the president of Coca-Cola to answer officially, before the United States Senate, the accusations levied against Coca-Cola.

"Not three years later, the president of Coca-Cola participated in selecting that same Mondale for membership in the Trilateral Commission I told you about in our first meeting. Then he selected him as vice president to President Carter.

"At the same time as Coca-Cola was accused of the theft of a handful of dollars from its workers, we read that it dedicated vast sums for charitable and cultural works ranging from an entire university budget to an important prize for artistic and literary creativity. It also presented a huge grant to the Brooklyn Museum in 1977 to rescue Egyptian pharaonic antiquities from collapse.

"Coca-Cola, according to statistics for 1978, distributes two hundred million bottles of soft drinks daily throughout the world, leaving tap water as its only rival. So, now we see it sponsoring projects for the desalinization of sea water, relying on the Aqua Chem Company that I bought a few years ago, in 1970 to be precise.

"These contradictions confused me, so I did several studies on Coca-Cola. Its policy was to remain committed to the two basic principles set down by its great founders. The first principle was to make every participant in the Coca-Cola enterprise rich and happy. The second was to restrict its energies to creating a single commodity: the well-known bottle.

"But the winds of change that blew in the early '60s forced a choice between the principles. In order not to sacrifice the first, Coca-Cola preferred to diversify its products. It began by producing other types of carbonated beverages, then extended its interests to farming peanuts, coffee, and tea. It had extensive holdings in that same state of Georgia where it was founded. Its farms neighbored those of the American president Carter, which perhaps was behind its involvement in public affairs, both domestic and international, and thus its policy of diversification grew all out of proportion.

"Obviously, this policy couldn't help but be successful. In this regard, it is sufficient to mention the return of the familiar bottle to both China and Egypt through the initiative in both countries of brave patriots, who acted on their principles.

"However, this success produced a strange phenomenon. With modern methods and lower production costs gained by relying on poorly paid migrant workers, Coca-Cola became the largest producer of fresh fruit in the Western world. But, sadly, it found itself forced to dump a large portion of the yield into the sea to keep the world market from collapsing.

"There was no solution to this problem except to continue diversifying. Coca-Cola exploited its great assets and expertise in the field of agriculture by sponsoring many nutritional programs in underdeveloped countries, among them a project to farm legumes in Abu

Dhabi, undertaken by its subsidiary, Aqua Chem. Likewise, it extensively researched the production of drinks
rich in proteins and other nutrients, thereby compen-
sating consumers for the surpluses it had been forced to
dump in the ocean."

I stopped a moment to catch my breath, then continued, "Thus, your honors, you see how diversification
provides—in the case of Coca-Cola—the key to unrav-
eling most of the phenomena linked to it. Through research, I found that this key can open many other locks.

"Indeed, a single look at the Arab reality is enough to
prove I am telling the truth. Right off, this reveals to us
the phenomenon of diversification in the outer trap-
pings of regimes (and this is certainly by design, because the essence of these regimes does not differ). It is
also revealed in the forms of political participation and
the corresponding slogans and goals.

"At one time all these regimes had applied one un-
changing means of persuasion to their people: imprisonment and torture. But diversification added other
sophisticated methods, from termination to television
to parliamentary councils.

"Once, all these regimes had espoused standard, un-
changing slogans. But they finally grasped the importance of changing these slogans and diversifying their
goals, alliances, and enmities from time to time.

"Due to the policy of diversification, this country's network of alliances, which were restricted in the past to the rest of the Arab peoples, were extended to now include the friendly country of Australia.

"Because of this policy, the Egyptians received plenty of the American, English, French, Italian, and German armaments that had long been withheld. In the '60s, the Egyptian market had been restricted to a single car, the Nasser/Fiat, which was assembled in local plants. Now, various imported makes of cars flooded into the market, arriving directly from their home factories.

"Formerly, housing projects, uniform in size and design, had been limited to the poorer classes. Now, they were offered to all classes, and acquired the utmost diversity, evolving into everything from tombs to luxurious high rises.

"The Egyptian cigarette is appropriate as a model for displaying and explaining the various, sometimes obscure, phenomena that accompany very complex processes such as diversification. You know, I'm sure, the strength of habit and the power of addiction. The Egyptians' devotion to their domestic brand reached a peak during the '60s, when imported cigarettes were banned. It was possible to merge several domestic brands into one, known as the Belmont, which satisfied a large proportion of the consumer market.

"This merger was the obstacle diversification faced in the cigarette industry. Overcoming it required exhaustive efforts along various lines. As a result, there were more periods when the Egyptian cigarette suddenly disappeared, and the consumer was forced to search for a foreign substitute.

"We can easily consider the shock of this sudden forced switch a cause of mental depression, especially since foreign cigarettes sell for twice the price of the local ones.

"Since the consumption of cigarettes in developing countries is more widespread than in other countries (the latter have forbidden advertising in order to alert their citizens to tobacco's link with cancer and now offer a variety of pleasures as alternative), the resulting depression is deeper and harder to treat, which causes foreign drug companies to recommend higher doses of powerful antidepressants for people in developing countries.

"This creates a new problem, which is addiction to these drugs. However, diversification itself offers the solution for this problem, for during a course of treatment, the doctor falls back on a continual change of medication in which the multiplicity of drugs is helpful.

"To consider depression itself, it is usually equivalent to a crossroads whose branches sometimes lead to sexual impotence, religious fanaticism, apathy, slovenliness, or insanity.

"Thus you see, gentlemen, how the process of diversification leads in and of itself to explaining the many phenomena in our contemporary life and how it joins them as links in a strong chain."

One of the members spoke hesitantly, looking at the Blond from time to time, "You set forth your point of view thoroughly and clearly. But there is something I would like to understand. As far as I'm concerned, you haven't dealt with the matter of tap water."

I answered at once in admiration, "You're right to raise this point, because it holds a special importance for all those engaged in scholarly research. It gives us a classic example of the mistakes in which researchers can get entangled.

"I knew the international sales volume of Coca-Cola and also that Egyptians are among the peoples who prefer tap water (in contrast to civilized people generally). This disparity induced me to link the return of this bottle to Egypt with the phenomena of the scarcity of tap water, its almost total disappearance during the day, and its dark, blackish color.

"However, I soon discovered that these phenomena mentioned above preceded the return of Coca-Cola by some years. Through research, I found that the tap had remained the main source of drinking water, from the '60s until the open-door policy went into effect and imported mineral water appeared. The change affecting tap water had begun at that moment, which was consistent with the results I found in similar circumstances, namely, the fate of the Egyptian cigarette.

"Reaching a conclusion and looking no further is among the perils normally facing researchers. However, continuing the research while guided by the same methodology, I was able to achieve a deeper understanding, which in turn revealed the links between a number of phenomena.

"To go on, for a long time Coca-Cola's desert irrigation projects were limited to a single category: desalinization of sea water. The October War provided a golden opportunity for it to diversify the tools of its trade by using the waters of the Nile to irrigate the Negev, facilitated by huge tunnels dug under the Suez Canal. Naturally, this sort of diversification leads to a scarcity of potable tap water, just as a lowering of the water level, through steadily increasing usage, causes dirt to permeate the water and change its color."

The Blond addressed me victoriously, "And you want us to believe you know all these things by your special effort with the newspapers?"

I answered, "Of course."

The officer-civilian or civilian-officer spoke for the first time. He was obviously wearing a wig. He addressed me firmly, "It would be best for you to tell the names of your accomplices and all the details of the conspiracy at once, before we force you. We are capable of undoing the knot in your tongue. Truly, due to the humanitarian principles that guide us, we are not inclined to resort to such methods, but the end justifies the means."

The old maid leaned toward me and said gently, "I don't believe we will be forced to go that far. He will talk when it's in his best interests."

My heart sank and I said, "I know the methods you refer to. Certainly they would force me to admit anything. But what I would admit in such a situation would not necessarily be the truth. You would always remain in doubt."

Silence fell over the hall and they began to exchange glances. I perceived—as the Committee would say—that this shot in the dark had hit home.

The Blond leaned toward the chairman and began a whispered exchange with him. Finally the latter spoke, "Perhaps it would be better if you withdrew for a little to consider the matter. You can go out now and we will summon you shortly to learn your decision."

I understood they wanted to get rid of me so they could deliberate freely. I left the hall and stood beside the elderly porter. I offered him a cigarette. He took it from me in silence and put it behind his ear. Meanwhile I lit up and inhaled greedily.

The hallway was empty. Light came from a large window in the opposite wall, which looked out on an empty courtyard. I smoked and peeked at the calm, resigned face of the porter sitting beside me. I wished for a moment that I were in his place, enjoying the same peace and tranquility. Then it occurred to me that his condition wasn't necessarily natural, that it could be the effect of some tranquilizer.

Whether that was the reason or whether he had picked up on how tight a spot I was in, he didn't reply when I tried to strike up a conversation by complaining of the heat.

I put out my cigarette, dropped the butt in the brass ashtray by the door, and leaned back against the wall. Unable to think, I looked ahead of me through the window, aware that I was staring out into nothingness.

After about half an hour the porter suddenly got up as though a secret message had reached him. He disappeared into the hall, reappeared at once, and signaled me to go in.

I entered nervously, hesitantly, hardly able to put one foot in front of the other. I stopped in the face of the stares surrounding me.

The old maid addressed me with her habitual graciousness, "What have you decided?"

"I don't have anything to add. I hope you appreciate the difficult, unnatural circumstances that hemmed me in," I said.

Suddenly ferocious, she said angrily, "Have it your own way then."

The chairman put some of the papers aside and said slowly, "Your intransigent attitude leaves us unable to find any rationalization for mercy or for granting your petition. Because of that—in our opinion—you deserve the harshest punishment on the books. This is our unanimous decision."

Some of them stood up and the others followed suit. They gathered their papers, pushed their chairs back, and headed for the inner door behind them. One after another they left the hall.

I continued watching their backs until the last of them had disappeared. I was alone—I, that picture of Stubby the ugly, and the funeral wreaths from all corners of the world.

I heard a noise at the main door to the hall. When I turned around I saw the porter looking at me questioningly. I walked toward him lethargically.

S I X

I stood outside until the porter had finished straightening up the hall and closing the windows. The moment he appeared in the doorway, I hurried over to offer him a cigarette and light it.

"Could you tell me the Committee's harshest punishment?" I asked him.

He shook his head and said firmly, "The Committee isn't a court."

"I know. What I'm looking for is the harshest punishment from their point of view."

"That depends on a lot of things."

"Naturally."

"Each situation is unique."

"Of course."

"In your case, which I have followed with great interest, there is no punishment more severe or rigorous than consumption."

Astonished, I asked, "Consumption? Who consumes and what does he consume?"

He looked at me a while, then getting up, said deliberately, "You consume yourself."

He and his chair disappeared into the hall. He closed the door behind him, leaving me alone in the dimly lit corridor. I waited for him to return in order to ask for more information, but he was gone a long time, so I decided to leave. I passed through empty anterooms, my footsteps echoing behind me, until I had left the building.

I took off aimlessly through the streets, my gaze wandering among passersby, storefronts, and entrances to houses. Even so, I was able to notice how most of the passersby had caught the urge to seek wealth and happiness. Crates of Coca-Cola were everywhere. Everyone stood behind them, grocers, doorkeepers, carpenters, and even pharmacists.

I felt thirsty and stopped in front of one of the vendors, whose shop was stocked exclusively with crates of these bottles. He had put a large, lidless cooler on the sidewalk. The thirsty crowded around it.

The cooler was full of bottles floating in water. Snatching one up, the vendor seemed in seventh heaven as he held it toward the outstretched hands. Before any hand grabbed it, he would remove the cap with the opener held ready in his other hand, then hurriedly pick up another one.

I noticed his hand holding a bottle out toward me. I quickly intervened before he popped the cap, asking, "Is it cold?"

Looking at me disapprovingly, he said, "As ice."

I touched the bottle and found it warm, so I said, "No, I'd like a cold one."

While making his displeasure with me clear, he held out the bottle toward the crowd. I reached out and rummaged among the bottles. I discovered that not only were most of them warm, but there was no sign of ice in the water. The vendor kept his eyes on the thirsty, who were wiping sweat from their brows and panting in the heat. He ministered to them with the warm bottles.

I watched them drink the magic liquid. They touched the bottles as though to assure themselves of their ability to distinguish hot and cold. Then, resigned, they swallowed the contents to the last drop and paid the price the vendor demanded. He had doubled the listed price on the pretext of the imaginary ice. He scowled and everyone paid it submissively.

I transferred my attention to the vendor, who was moving energetically and somewhat aggressively. I guessed he would attain his ambition quickly; the store would soon be filled with foreign cigarettes and candy, then with other imported commodities, including cassettes, tape recorders, and canned goods.

I was caught up in my thoughts and didn't notice what was happening until there was a warm opened bottle in my hand. I automatically raised it to my lips.

I paid the price the others had paid and continued walking in a leisurely fashion to the bus stop. I stood with the others until the "Carter" bus came.

The rationale behind using the name of the American president for this type of bus can't be attributed to its particular shape, which resembles a long, sad-faced worm, or to its unusual length, or to the great roar it makes as it runs, or to its higher fares (five times the usual fare), or to its being made in the USA. Rather, it has to do with the insignia on its side, right next to the door, which consists of an American flag emblazoned with two hands clasped in friendship.

In all likelihood, this insignia is the source of the people's delight in the buses' appearance during the last two years or so. They consider the buses the herald of the promised prosperity, which has been so long in coming. They seem prepared to overlook the noise on the grounds that noise is something commonplace in an underdeveloped country like ours. Higher fares are overlooked on the grounds that world prices are rising, and the thick polluting exhaust on the grounds that environmental pollution is only a problem in developed countries. The absence of bars and straps, which leaves the standing passengers swaying and dancing, is excused on the premise that our dull life needs some recreation.

However, it wasn't a week before the buses developed strange symptoms. Their interior support had begun to collapse and the rivets holding the walls to pop out. The automatic doors stuck open and the wall panels fell off. The rubber gaskets in the windows were torn and the screws holding the dashboard came off, revealing the inner workings.

The longer the papers remained silent about these wondrous phenomena, the more the explanations proliferated. They ranged from citing poor maintenance as the cause, to citing the hard use buses are put to in our country and the drivers' inadequacy and carelessness.

But other makes of buses that were in circulation along with the "Carter" bus were still in good condition, although it had been years since they were put into operation. Some of them were even assembled in Egyptian workshops. All this cast doubt on the soundness of these inferences.

Perhaps because of the frustration the common people felt at their inability to explain this phenomenon or perhaps because in every time and place people alter nouns and adjectives so that their vocabulary matches their level of education and limited awareness, they soon called the buses mentioned above "Tartar."

This linguistic development drew my attention at the time. I consulted dictionaries until I found that "tartar" is among the oldest words in Arabic and means false pride. From this derives the word "taratur," meaning a conical dervish hat, which is also a slur applied to a weak wretch. But "tartar" as a noun means filtered wine dregs and thence, generally, has come to mean colloquially "to take a leak."

In light of what had happened to me lately, which stimulated my mind and drew me into probing phenomena and attempting to explain them, it is natural that my interest shifted from the linguistic aspect to the essence of this phenomenon itself. I intended to get on the "Tartar" several times, and while riding, painstakingly examine its makeup. But my findings made things more ambiguous.

I discovered the bus was made of the worst and cheapest components, from the outer frame and right down to the nails used to hold down the floorboards. It didn't make sense that the bus would be allowed to operate in this condition on the streets of New York, even in the black ghettos. Nor would it make sense for it to be produced especially for us. Like the foreign drugs, I couldn't imagine that the industry of the world's richest and strongest country could produce, even by design, such a poor-quality product. Even if the United States sent us the motors and nothing else, and the buses were then assembled in our country, this would still not be an explanation, since we've had industrial assembly since the '60s. A fortunate few still hold on to powerful, sturdy buses produced in Egyptian factories.

At this thought, my nose, well trained by the odor of old newspapers, began to quiver in excitement.

However, the developments in my relationship with the Committee wouldn't give me the opportunity to reach significant conclusions. To me, as to others, the matter became an unfathomable mystery.

I remembered all this as I worked my way in between jostling passengers near the back exit of the bus. I searched in vain for something to hold onto while boarding. There was an enormously fat woman in front of me. She climbed on with difficulty and found a spot inside. I was behind her when the bus suddenly set off and she lost her balance.

She reached out to cling to one of the metal poles, but it bent under her weight so that she almost fell on her face. She clung to me. Meanwhile I was busy taking out the fare the conductor demanded. I had spread my legs to brace myself and avoid falling.

The woman regained her balance and moved forward. She moved in spite of herself because of the bus' motion and the vibration of the floorboards, which had cracked and separated each from the other in many places.

Lately, preoccupied, I had not left my apartment much. I had not had a chance to ride the "Tartar" even once. I noticed immediately how the passengers' reactions had changed.

Early in the bus' service, the dancing motion that occurred had called forth a shy smile from all the riders, whether sitting or standing.

Today I noticed that the violence of the dance had increased, tearing the bus apart, breaking up the walls and floor, and completely destroying the riders' delight in the dancing.

Since they were looking, oblivious, at the ads decorating the streets, it appeared to me that they were preoccupied with other things. These ads were about international inventions in all fields. They looked at the late-model cars equipped with new features to protect passengers from noise, dirt, heat, cold, and the eyes of others, so that the vehicles resemble small armored cars.

I continued to look around at the thin, exhausted faces, stopping at a middle-aged man absorbed in some less-than-cheerful thought which was reflected on his features. He was smoking nervously. Beside him sat a youth with straightened hair and a gold chain around his neck. Another man clasped his hands greedily over a passport. There was a woman with wide-framed glasses, violet colored to match her dress, and a wristwatch shaped like a spaceship.

Sitting beside her was a sad-faced man proudly holding a package from which wafted the aroma of fish. He must have gotten it on sale in some corner of the city. Behind him, a neatly dressed man was nodding off, even though he was armed with all the modern devices: glasses with tinted lenses, a watch with a calculator, an annual calendar and alarm, and a Samsonite briefcase.

My eyes stopped on two female passengers sitting next to each other. As though withdrawing completely from our miserable world, their bodies were swathed from head to foot in dark baggy clothes with holes for the eyes. They seemed more like owls, or two frightened aliens from outer space.

I decided that all of them were oppressed and humiliated, but had remarkable powers of endurance. Absorbed in thinking about this aspect of the situation, I didn't notice someone had come up beside me until he stepped on my toes.

I was standing next to a plump, middle-aged woman.

Almost plastered against her back was a giant in a shirt partially unbuttoned so as to show off his chest. He was looking out the window, feigning absentmindedness. The woman moved ceaselessly in an effort to keep away from him, which made her bump against me.

I made as much room for her as I could in the crowd. I watched—as did most of those around us—the minute space between his leg and her behind. He had bent his knee forward a little to aggravate her. I could only raise my eyes to him in complete disapproval.

I'm the first to admit I have a thing for that protruding part of the female body and am an aficionado of stolen moments in a crowd. From my point of view, this behavior, which some may condemn and which arises from our reality and independent character, is nothing other than an Arab substitute for Western dancing in which people pursue such business face-to-face.

But our national substitute fulfills a more complex role than the mere release of repressed desires. It is a successful way of fighting the boredom arising from overcrowding and frequent long delays in streets jammed with private cars. Likewise, for me, it is an important means of releasing tension and one method of acquiring knowledge.

A woman is a mysterious creature, the object of a thousand speculations, especially if she appears haughty and hostile, until, at the light brush of a leg, she suddenly reveals herself by indicating her consent or objection.

However, for this practice I set myself an important rule which distills the essence of the ensuing pleasure. This rule was also in accordance with one of the moral principles I had imposed on myself: to avoid hurting others. The first or second brush of my leg against anyone's behind suffices for a connoisseur like myself to tell whether the woman shares my secret pleasure. If not, I lose interest in her.

My principle made me disapprove of his behavior toward the woman. More than once she had indicated in no uncertain terms that she disliked the proposition the giant was making by repeatedly brushing her with his leg.

It was apparent he subscribed to other moral principles. He ignored her distress and attempts to avoid him. Indeed, he persisted in touching her, which made her protest openly.

She suddenly turned to him and said agitatedly, "I wish you'd cut it out."

He was astonished, then exploded loudly, "Cut what out, lady?"

"You know what I mean!" she snapped.

Silence fell in the bus. The passengers glanced toward them, smiles of amusement and enjoyment on most lips.

The man raised his hand, slapped her face roughly, and shouted, "You whore!"

The woman sank onto the passenger beside her, pressed her hand to her cheek, and burst out sobbing. None of the passengers moved a muscle.

The giant spoke without addressing anyone in particular, "The way some people behave these days!"

I don't usually let myself get into situations I'm not physically up to. However, since the morning when I hadn't been able to speak my mind to the Committee, I had been seething and I hadn't even benefited from my meekness. On top of that, I hadn't been able to turn the tables on the Coca-Cola vendor who had robbed me. Likewise, the crowd and the heat grated on my nerves. In short, matters came to a head.

It's not inconceivable that I drew courage from facing one person rather than the whole Committee. Since they had been following the matter from the beginning and knew full well what had happened, I may also have been encouraged by imagining that all the passengers would leap to my aid. Perhaps out of religious or moral considerations they would condemn the giant's sexual behavior, or disapprove of his striking a defenseless woman, or simply stand by the truth.

I found myself unexpectedly addressing the giant, "The woman has a valid complaint."

He stared in disbelief and asked threateningly, "What are you getting at?"

I said firmly, "I saw you plastering yourself against her. When she didn't respond, you should have left her alone."

"Liar!" he screamed. "I think you two are in cahoots."

I looked at the bystanders and persisted, "I'm not the only one who saw what happened."

Suddenly everyone looked the other way, some at things along the route, whereas others just turned their backs. My adversary didn't wait for anyone to take his part, but decided to finish the matter quickly. He threw a knockout punch and hit me in the face, throwing me onto some seated passengers.

Before I could recover from the effects of this blow, which made me see stars and made the world spin before my eyes, he pulled me by my forearms and shoved me again. My shoulder hit one of the metal poles. I lost my balance. I saw I would fall on my face, so I stretched out my right hand. My weight landed full on it as I hit the floor.

I felt a sharp pain in my forearm. The giant had plunged headlong after me, cursing my forefathers. Two of the passengers got between us. Several tried to soothe him, as though it was I who had acted unjustly.

I heard someone say to him, "Calm down. A cat in heat and a fag. Your virility aroused them and they picked a quarrel with you. Why sweat blood over them?"

While this exchange was going on, the bus came to a stop. The passengers freed me and pushed me toward the door saying, "Get off while the getting's good."

Automatically I got off the bus and stood in the street looking at my disheveled clothing. When I tidied myself up, the pain shooting up my arm made me notice the strange position it was in, twisted at the elbow. The bones of the joint were visibly out of place.

I hurried to look for the nearest hospital where I could have it treated cheaply at an outpatient clinic. I found one, but the doctor wasn't in. I waited so long I got fed up. If it hadn't been for the pain that seared through my forearm at the slightest movement, I would have gone home without thinking twice about its strange position.

After almost an hour, a medic approached me and let me know that it was too late for the doctor to show up. If I urgently needed him, he was now at his nearby private practice.

I tipped him for his advice and went at once to the doctor's clinic. After paying five pounds at the door, I entered a fashionable, air-conditioned room where soft European music played.

Having examined me thoroughly, the doctor relieved my mind by saying that the bones had shifted out of position at the elbow but that it was not at all serious. By pressing with his hand, which hurt, he pushed the bones back into place, then wrote me a prescription for some pain killers.

I set off for my apartment, climbed wearily to the seventh floor, and immediately took refuge in bed. I gave myself up to a deep sleep until the pain in my arm drew me back to consciousness. I tried some of the pain killers, to no avail. Although the pain wasn't extreme, it was persistent. I had a lot of things I needed to do right away, which, thanks to the little time left me, required my total concentration. When the pain continued into the next day and prevented me from thinking, I was forced to go back to the doctor.

I was surprised when the medic who admitted the patients asked me to pay one pound. I said, "But I paid a whole five pounds only yesterday."

"I know," he said. "That was the fee for the exam. What I am asking now is the fee for a consultation."

"This is the first time I've heard of charging for a consultation," I said in amazement.

He didn't bother to answer me, but merely pointed his finger at a sign on the wall without even turning his head.

The sign—which I hadn't noticed before—proclaimed that patients are allowed one follow-up visit within a week of the diagnosis at a fee of one pound.

I said agitatedly, "But this is exploitation, pure and simple!"

He took no notice of my argument, but said coldly, "This is our system. Take it or leave it."

The patients and their companions, seated nearby, had silently followed our discussion. Their poker faces betrayed no shadow of their thoughts. In front of them I was embarrassed to appear so concerned with such a paltry sum as one pound, so in the end, humiliated, I paid what was requested.

Because my visit was for advice and not a diagnosis, my turn came quickly. I stalked into the doctor's cubicle and sat next to his desk. At once I noticed his pallor and the strange luster of his skin.

He surprised my by saying, "So in your opinion I'm a profiteer?"

I was amazed at how he could know what his assistant and I had talked about. My heartbeat sped up immediately, but I didn't back down. I answered, "Do you have some other name for what you do?"

"I thought I was performing a humanitarian service."

"Listen, you demanded a whole five pounds from me for a service that costs almost nothing in a public hospital, which is where you ought to be. What's humanitarian in that?"

"A clinic like this is expensive," he said. "Furthermore, there's no hospital whose services you can trust."

I said hysterically, "You and your ilk have been the ruin of public hospitals to the advantage of private shops. You have conspired to fleece anyone with the bad luck to fall into your hands."

He stiffened and said disdainfully, "It's my right to set the fee for the services I offer in any way I see fit."

"And I'm entitled to free treatment from you," I said.

He raised his eyebrows in surprise, "How so?"

Gesturing with my good arm to include the doctor as well as the furniture, the air conditioner, the sound system, and the medical equipment, I leaned over the desk, saying, "None of this has resulted from your unique genius. You and your ilk benefit from a system of inherited privileges that over time have been wrested from me and from others, our fathers and forefathers. Above and beyond this, you are from the generation that had a free education, a free ride on me and others like me."

He stood up, shaking with anger. "Enough. I don't want to argue with you. I want you to leave my clinic now. Your kind has no right to my services."

As he pressed the buzzer firmly with both hands, I

said, "I admit I made a mistake in coming to you. As soon as you return the pound I paid today, I'll leave."

He said superciliously, "My time is valuable and you've wasted too much of it already. Therefore, I don't owe you anything. If you don't go now, I'll have the medic toss you out in the street."

The medic who appeared in the door was a strapping young man and I was afraid the incident on the bus would be repeated. I got up slowly and said, "I'll go. But I know what to do about my pound. We still have law and order around here."

Naturally, I didn't believe that, but it was a way of saving face, helping me face the critical looks that met me outside and the insults with which the medic escorted me to the door.

I walked along seething, hardly noticing anything around me. I wasn't aware of myself until a woman bumped my forearm and it hurt. At that point I started walking toward my apartment, picking my way with difficulty around the ditches, the dirt, the garbage that nobody has an incentive to remove or even complain about, and the piles of imported goods and crates of Coca-Cola filling the sidewalk.

I began to look around at the people who were crowding the streets, shopping enthusiastically, cracking seeds, and listening to songs. I blamed myself that my fear of pain had exposed me to humiliation by the physician. In fact, when considering the fate awaiting me, it hadn't been worth the effort.

I bought enough food for a few days. I told the doorman to tell anyone who asked for me that I was away. I climbed to my apartment.

There were a few things I had to take care of right away. I got busy at this, even though moving my arm was painful. I went through my old papers and put them in order. I spent some pleasant moments, although they were tinged with sorrow, in going over my accomplishments and the resulting comments and reverberations. Old government applications, tickets, letters, bills, and receipts helped me trace the course I had taken since I stood on my own feet.

I lingered over a picture of my father. I contemplated his legacy, laden with pain, negative attitudes, and delusions, and also laden with the hopes he had pinned on me. Time hadn't allowed him to witness the outcome. Thank God he wouldn't see my fate.

I spent a whole day sorting through pictures of individuals who had crossed my path and women I had been linked with, all of whom I had pinned my hopes on at different stages. I dwelt on everything that had combined to shatter those hopes, looking one last time for where things had gone wrong.

Naturally, this preoccupation stirred up certain feelings. So I got out my porno books and with the aid of my fantasies and memories sought to live for the last time those charged moments, during which life floods every cell of the body and a caress anywhere arouses waves of ecstasy that inevitably crest.

The following day I was entirely occupied with my old diaries and the notes I had made in moments suffused with suffering and hope. At one time their possibilities seemed limitless, but now they appeared faded, yet still tinged with sorrow. The great plans I had at one time mapped out enthusiastically and the ensuing frustrations leaped out at me from the yellowing pages.

Numerous quotations I had copied from my readings at various times stared out at me. Most of them spoke of the ideal way of life. I spent hours staring at these lines by Mayakovsky, which he most likely spoke shortly before his tragic end:

I hope I trust the day shall never dawn
when I stoop to the shame of being sensible . . .

It's then that one wants to rise—rise
and address time, time and history,
and all creation . . .

His fate reminded me of my tragedy. I recalled the events that had happened to me since I had prepared myself for my first interview with the Committee. I reviewed the stages of the whole experience and how it had opened my eyes—completely—to the whole dreadful truth, even though this came too late.

When I visualized the details of the last interview, I regretted my complaisance and how, before the whole Committee, I had lost the glibness and courage which were part of me when dealing with individuals, like Stubby, the giant on the bus, and the physician.

I was engaged in finding an explanation for this phenomenon, when, after some examination, I realized it was rooted in the distant past, in the first test I had ever taken, at just a few years of age, and each time thereafter when I stood naked before the cold, indifferent eyes of ruthless people who belonged to a world other than mine. The life of each of them revolves in an independent sphere, not dependent in any way on the outcome of any confrontation between us, which is contrary to my own case.

I wished I was standing before the Committee members again, so that I could make them listen to me. I imagined myself facing them confidently. I went on to pick precise, exact expressions. I got carried away. Suddenly I stood up, put an empty tape in the recorder, and set it on the table. I faced it as if it were the Committee.

My voice rang out strong and steady in the empty room. "I committed—from the beginning—unpardonable errors. I shouldn't have stood before you, but against you. Every noble effort on this earth should be aimed at eliminating you.

"Let me quickly add that I am not so naïve as to imagine that were this achieved, the matter would end there. By the very nature of things, a new Committee would take your place. No matter the beauty of its plans or the perfection of its goals, corruption would soon set in. Even if it started out as a symbol, it would become an obstacle, and sooner or later it in turn would have to be eliminated.

"From my investigations of history and cases similar to mine, I perceived that via this very process—an ongoing process of change and transformation—your group will gradually lose what authority it has, while the power of those like me to confront and resist it will grow.

"However, unfortunately, I won't be here when that takes place, because of the fate allotted me, a fate deriving on the one hand from my ambitions, which exceeded my potential, and my quixotic search for knowledge and, on the other hand, from my entanglement in a reckless but inevitable attempt to challenge your Committee at an unsuitable time and place. But what alleviates my sorrow is my confidence in what will eventually happen, for this is the logic of history and the nature of life."

I didn't exaggerate, and I didn't get carried away talking to the tape recorder. Now, as I considered everything through my impartial eyes, I totaled the gains and losses and found myself not regretting the fate awaiting me. In comparison with other fates—at least in my generation—there was nothing to be ashamed of. What made me truly sorry was that I would miss the great day. But this in itself had no real significance since I was convinced it would come.

When I reached this conclusion, I felt a strange peace of mind which filled my heart with a tranquility I had rarely known. I spent a few intoxicated moments, the likes of which I had only experienced when listening to music. I wanted to prolong these moments right to the end, so I got out my tape recordings, which I took pride in. I leafed through them for a long time, passing over those notable for their delicate, pleasant melodies, such as Mozart and Grieg, or those composers who expressed sorrow, such as Schubert and Tchaikovsky. My soul likewise rejected the enchanted world of Berlioz and Scriabin and the solemn metaphysics of Mahler and Sibelius.

My choice finally came to rest on Cesar Franc, in whom the splendor of doubt evolves into the bliss of certainty, Carl Orff, who erupts with vigor and conflict, Beethoven, who sings of victory and joy after pain, and Shostakovich, who blended all of this with mockery.

Darkness had fallen. I put the recordings of these great geniuses within reach of my hand. I took my favorite place behind the desk, at the final wall of the apartment.

I proceeded to listen to the music, whose notes rang throughout the room. I stayed in my place, tranquil, elated, until dawn.

Then I lifted my wounded arm to my mouth and began to consume myself.

A F T E R W O R D

Modern modes of critical analysis have taught us to look closely at the various ways in which works of fiction achieve closure. With the strictures of Henry James in mind regarding so-called happy endings—marriages, inheritances, discoveries of long-lost relatives, not to mention the alternatives proposed by John Fowles in his well-known novel *The French Lieutenant's Woman*—we are now accustomed to encounters with a wide variety of strategies whereby a novel's narrator chooses to terminate his activities. With "Then I lifted my wounded arm to my mouth and began to consume myself," the final sentence of Sonallah Ibrahim's novel, *The Committee,* the reader comes face-to-face with a particularly shocking example of this variety, in that the narrator recounts the initial stage of a process whereby he will disappear by self-consumption.

The process he describes is, as we have already learned from the narrative, a direct consequence of the dreadful sentence that has been passed on him by "the Committee" that gives its name to the novel's title. The exact purview of this "Committee" is never mentioned; it is just "the Committee." It has, the narrator informs us, great importance and extensive authority, and yet "officially it [doesn't] exist." However, the narrator's reactions to a summons to appear before it and the various ways in which its procedures manage to impinge on and interfere with his lifestyle, professional conduct, and research agenda all convey to the reader a truly disturbing picture of an organization—in fact, a society—in which individuality and difference are considered subversive. In this regard, Sonallah Ibrahim can be regarded as a true peer of Franz Kafka in his ability to make use of a disarmingly undramatic level of discourse to convey a reality that is genuinely disturbing in its routine callousness. The mindless bureaucracy that appears to be all-powerful succeeds, almost effortlessly, in creating a general atmosphere of paranoia within which the individual is to be crushed.

Indeed, the Committee in Ibrahim's novel reaches a unanimous decision, one that condemns the narrator to "the harshest punishment on the books," that process of self-consumption with which the narrative concludes.

The way in which Sonallah Ibrahim's masterful use of discourse style manages to convey this atmosphere is one of the great achievements of this work of his, as well as others.

The narrator of this unsettling story self-identifies as an Egyptian. However, the Committee itself does not use Arabic as its language. It is further described as being made up of civilians and military personnel. Among prominently mentioned members is a blond man who, among other disarming procedures, conducts an investigation of the narrator's private parts in order to assess the veracity of charges of impotence that have been made. The all-important symbolic power of this unspecified bureaucratic machine thus brings some broader concerns to Sonallah Ibrahim's novelistic reflection on Egypt. Thus, the first chapter may indeed concern itself entirely with the narrator's initial confrontation with the Committee (and, on a biographical note, it is worth pointing out that this chapter was published as a separate piece in the journal *Al-Fikr al-mu'asir* [May 1979], some two years before the appearance of the complete work). However, in subsequent chapters, the narrator follows the Committee's directives by undertaking a research project on a famous figure in society. In his decision to examine the career of the personality known simply as "the Doctor," the narrator inevitably finds himself introducing a more chronologically and politically focused mode to the underlying commentary of the text. The first resort, needless to say, is to the archives of the press. From this source it emerges that "the Doctor" is a veritable paragon of the era during the 1970s when President Sadat radically transformed the bases of the Egyptian economy by introducing his "open-door" economic policies *(infitah* in Arabic). Readers will, no doubt, immediately notice the way that the entire narrative of *The Committee* seems almost obsessed with the "Coca-Cola" culture. The economic phenomenon of globalism, viewed as such a modern and progressive development within the context of the market-driven societies of the Western world, emerges from within the third-world perspective provided by an ironic reading of this novel as an alien import, one whose benefits for the vast majority of people are far from obvious. In his blandly uncritical commentary, the narrator shows "the Doctor" to be socially and economically remote from that "vast majority." Having already become rich even in the period before the October War with Israel in 1973 (the so-called crossing of the Suez Canal [Al-'Ubur]), he has since become a maximal beneficiary of the new entrepreneurial trends in Egypt, having made opportunistic use of the moment to parlay construction interests and even arms dealing into a position of wealth and prestige. Such is his renown that, as the narrator discovers during a visit to the American Embassy library where he is able to peruse issues of *Time* and *Newsweek,* "the Doctor" is the subject of an elaborate profile that includes accounts of his poor background, his frequent use of "connections" (including the marriage of his own daughter), and his close linkages to important figures both inside and outside Egypt.

The ringing endorsement of "the Doctor's" personal qualities and achievements undertaken by the narrator in response to a challenge from the Committee (and particularly the member nicknamed "Stubby") becomes, in Sonallah Ibrahim's skillful hands, a stinging indictment of the values of an entire class in Egypt that has chosen to enrich itself at the expense of its fellow citizens. The author's ire at the increasing polarization of society expressed in this powerful fashion can be placed alongside that of his fellow Egyptian novelist, Naguib Mahfouz, in the novels that he too penned during this period, among them *Malhamat al-Harafish* (1977; *The Harafish,* 1994), *Al-Baqi min al-Zaman Sa'ah (Just One Hour Left,* 1982), and, above all, *Yawm Qutil al-Za'im* (1985; *The Day the Leader Was Killed,* 1989).

The author of *The Committee,* Sonallah Ibrahim, was born in 1937 and educated both in Egypt and the Soviet Union. Like many other leftist writers whose careers span the course of the Egyptian revolution, he suffered the horrors of imprisonment and forced labor between 1959 and 1964. The work that first attracted the attention of critics both inside and outside Egypt was a direct consequence of this experience, the short novel *Tilka al-Ra'ihah* (1966 [incomplete], 1986 [complete]; *The Smell of It,* 1971). Like *Al-Lajnah (The Committee)*, it is narrated in a terse, detached style that only serves to emphasize the incredible degree of tedium and tension felt by a recently released political prisoner forced to be at home for a police check every few hours. In an astute study of Ibrahim's works, Samia Mehrez points out that a succession of works that he has penned can be viewed as a running commentary on the book in Egypt and therefore on the general state of civil liberties in the majority of countries within the Arab world region *(Egyptian Writers Between History and Fiction,* 1994, pp. 39–57). In 1974 Ibrahim had published *Najmat Aghustus* (August Star), a sardonic account of the officially orchestrated glorification of the high dam project in Aswan, but with *Al-Lajnah (The Committee)* there is once again a return to the all-too-real world of interrogations and constraints that are, it would appear, the necessary implements of such a closely monitored society. Mehrez convincingly demonstrates the way in which *The Committee* can be viewed as Ibrahim's commentary on the atmosphere of suspicion and institutional harassment that are so clearly represented by the tortuous publication history of *Tilka al-Ra'ihah* (and the complete edition was eventually to be published in Morocco). Still later comes *Bayrut, Bayrut* (Beirut, Beirut, 1984), a novel that, against the background of the Lebanese civil war [1975–88], explores, and indeed debunks, the reputation of Lebanon as the liberal center of Arabic book publication. Two novels of the 1990s, *Dhat* (1992) and *Sharaf* (1997) reveal Sonallah Ibrahim as a widely recognized craftsman of contemporary fiction, a member of a distinguished generation of novelists who, working in the mighty shadow of Mahfouz, continue their experiments with texts and styles in order to reflect their views of his society and world in excitingly new ways.

In terse and undecorated prose of great subtlety, Sonallah Ibrahim's *The Committee* introduces English readers to a world that has already become familiar to us through the works of Kafka and other portrayers of the bureaucratic and totalitarian mind. However, it has new and important things to tell us. For, in an era in which the term "globalism" has become a catchword used to imply, reflect, and promote what is widely viewed as the way of the future, it is a salutary corrective to read an accomplished narrative from another cultural tradition and world area, one indeed that is a target of global trends and that, like many others, views the alleged benefits involved in this entire process with a wary and often jaundiced eye. It is merely part of Sonallah Ibrahim's artistry that he manages to couch such notions in a narrative of such cogent subtlety.

November 2000   Roger Allen

Sonallah Ibrahim is an Egyptian novelist and a major literary figure in the Arab world. He has published short stories, historical and scientific children's books, translations of American and German fiction, and seven novels, including *Tilka al-ra'iha (The Smell of It)*, *Beirut-Beirut,* and *Warda.*

Mary St. Germain is head of the Near East section at the University of Washington Libraries.

Charlene Constable studied Arabic at the University of Washington and has traveled in Syria, Jordan, and Egypt. She has a long-standing interest in translation.

Other titles in Middle East Literature in Translation

The Author and His Doubles: Essays on Classic Arabic Culture
Abdelfattah Kilito; Michael Cooperson, trans.

A Cup of Sin: Selected Poems
Simin Behbahani; Farzaneh Milani and Kaveh Safa, trans.

In Search of Walid Masoud: A Novel
Jabra Ibrahim Jabra; Roger Allen and Adnan Haydar, trans.

Three Tales of Love and Death
Out el Kouloub; Nayra Atiya, trans.

Women without Men: A Novella
Shahrnush Parsipur; Kamran Talattof and Jocelyn Sharlet, trans.

Yasar Kemal on His Life and Art
Eugene Lyons Hébert and Barry Tharaud, trans.

Zanouba: A Novel
Out el Kouloub; Nayra Atiya, trans.